My Girlfriend, the Witch-Queen

M. P. Smythe

O&H Books LLC

Cover designed by MiblArt. miblart.com

Published by O&H Books LLC.

eBook ISBN: 978-1-959703-03-7

Print ISBN: 978-1-959703-02-0

CONTENTS

Dedication   V

Check out the prologue, free!   VI

1. Dinner Date with the Witch-Queen   1

2. Companion to the Crown   21

3. The Marathon   45

4. The Price   51

5. The Flames of Hope   67

6. Decadence   87

7. Consequences   105

8. The Witch-Boyfriend   113

9. An Omelet of People   123

10. The Mason Foundation   139

11. Money   155

12. Intrigue   173

13. Revenge   189

14. Empire   205

15. The Answer   219

Acknowledgments   223

Want more Witch-Queen?   225

About the Author   227

To Mary, the Queen of Heaven
To Mom and Dad, who showed me opposites really can attract
And to A. R. K. Watson, who told me I could do it, and S. R. Crickard, who told
me I should.

CHECK OUT THE PROLOGUE, FREE!

See where it all began in *The Prototype Diagram!*

1

DINNER DATE WITH THE WITCH-QUEEN

"**C**alm down, man," I said to my reflection in the mirror. "It's just a fancy meal. We'll eat it, she'll be happy, and Lumberton will get the help it needs. It'll all work out."

My reflection didn't agree. I saw fear in my olive eyes, an accidental cut on my clean-shaven face, and a slightly-too-small suit that was a steal at 100 Imperial Marks, which also probably cost less than the tip where I was going.

At least I wouldn't be paying for it.

I held my head. "How did I end up here?" I asked my reflection.

I had seen the throne room on TV, after watching the audiences weekly on INN to prepare. But being there in person, ten days ago, had been another matter entirely.

Unlike on TV, I could barely see the Witch-Queen herself, just a small woman in a wide black dress, sitting on top of a diamond throne. Above was her coat of arms, below a black granite dais.

"Ornate" did not begin to describe the wide, spacious hall. Black banners hung from the marble walls and ceiling on diamond-tipped golden rods, and I wondered how much that decor had cost. Sweltering daylight shone through the open diamond windows, and there was no air conditioning, only the faint salty smell of the ocean. None of this was remotely expensive compared to the fact the Capital was suspended over the Mediterranean through billions of marks' worth of gravity generators and nuclear reactors, a city built entirely by and for the Witch-Queen.

As the long winding line approached her, I looked around for anything that would ground me in this crazy place. The ground itself, a marble-white floor, was covered with a massive pattern inscribed in grooves: concentric circles and geometric shapes, labeled with mixtures of symbols and characters in languages long dead. Courtiers in bespoke suits or fancy gowns stood at attention behind the two tables to the side. Several magisters wore what had once been considered a magician's garb, back when magic was make-believe. The Imperatrix Mundi had conquered the world, but she had not killed all of the Old Magisterium.

"I will consider the matter. Next!" said the Witch-Queen in a soft soprano. The man with the crying child hurried off.

My stomach knotted.

As we approached, petitioner by petitioner, I could pick out details on her coat of arms, or at least the motto at the bottom: *Per Aspera Ex Luna*. Although the Witch-Queen spoke with a faint British accent, no one really knew where she came from, other than "the Moon." She didn't seem too concerned by any petition, but I wondered if that was a form of official detachment or just boredom.

As I saw her sharp eyes carefully examine each petitioner, I decided she was just detached. I had counted six sob stories so far, and she had—no, chose—to do this every Friday, inviting a weekly torrent of human misery and despairing hope. Every Imperial citizen had a right to one audience with her per lifetime.

And this was mine.

An unmanned typewriter rattled away, recording everything that was said. "I will consider the matter," she repeated to the petitioner before me. I could hear her perfectly—the room was deathly still aside from the typewriter, and had amazing acoustics. "Next!"

I gulped.

She consulted no schedule as she greeted me. "Michael Mason of Lumberton?"

"Yes, Your Imperial Majesty," I replied, stepped forward, and bowed deeply to the edge of the carpet before her. Deeper than before the tabernacle at church, the irrelevant thought entered my brain. But I could go there any time! I had spent months training for this one moment. It was our only chance. After all, the Witch-Queen only granted one audience per citizen per lifetime.

I looked up at her, and lost my train of thought. I could barely breathe, after all.

I had thought propaganda artists, or her daemons, had done their best to prettify her. They didn't need to. She was small, yes, but looked almost girly in her youthful face, maybe around my age. That face was pale white with soft features, her only exposed skin contrasting with the all-covering elaborate black velvet dress and immaculate white gloves. Her hair was the right shade of auburn, though I couldn't see much of it, because it was full of diamonds and the Imperial Diadem.

She met my eyes with her own, sharp, piercing and emerald. "Well?"

D'oh! I snapped out of it and hastily began my well-practiced spiel. "Ma'am, our village relies on an old well system for water. Recently, we discovered a kind of trapped daemon inside, and it has become unsafe to draw from it. If you would kindly deign to remove it, we would be forever in your debt."

"Can you move the village?" she asked.

The Elders and the Mayor had argued for hours over what my response to that question ought to be, but we had finally decided honesty was the best policy. I kept my voice steady. "Theoretically, ma'am. But we would lose anything we can't move. We don't have the resources to reconstruct an entire village. And—it is our home, ma'am."

"I see," she said, looking into my eyes as if searching for the slightest deception. I was going to melt, and not from the summer heat. Then she smiled slightly, as if on a whim. "Is that all?"

"That is all."

"Thank you for being brief. I will consider the matter. Next!"

I bowed and walked out, hoping against hope that this was enough. The Palace didn't publish statistics on how many petitions the Imperatrix granted. But after seeing her, I clung to a little hope that mine would be one.

I lay on my bed in the expensive hotel room, exhausted. My once-in-a-lifetime interaction felt like it had lasted two lifetimes.

What the hell did that smile mean?

I couldn't get it, or the rest of her face, out of my mind. If I had bumped into her at the library I would have started praying for the courage to go up and talk to her. She was just that gorgeous.

"You're going nuts, man," I told myself. "Like she'd seriously want a boyfriend." No, I was going to stop it there. We would never meet again, and God willing, she would save our village.

Speaking of which, I decided I should call home. They had to all have been watching INN, probably since daybreak their time, to see my audience.

I flipped open my cellphone. For the Witch-Queen's faults, she had standardized nearly everything worldwide, so my plan still worked even in the Capital. Through the cracked screen I could still see Mom's congratulatory text:

`You did awesome. I love you.`

I texted back.

`I'm exhausted.`

Someone knocked at the door. Room service? The idea of having *anyone* to be a servant was foreign to me. I walked up and opened the door—to see a magister in an expensive suit waiting outside with a solemn expression. "Michael Mason?"

Oh no dear God this is the answer isn't it? "That's me," I said, my mind shooting off in every direction at once like a pack of dogs with ADHD.

"Her Imperial Majesty wishes to tell you that she will listen to your request in more detail if you dine with her ten days from now."

Oh no. Oh *no.*

"Yes, sir," I stammered. "Tell her I'd be pleased. Delighted, even!"

"Very good." He gave me a card and a look of disinterested pity, then bowed and left.

I closed the door, went back inside and sat down. Deep breathing. Deep breathing. This was progress. Progress that could end in my death, yes, but progress. Besides, only like three or four people had ever died of poisons intended for the Witch-Queen. Officially, at any rate. You had to figure she didn't release the exact numbers or no one would be her food tester any more. Kyle claimed the actual number was five hundred, but he believed everything.

Whatever. Five or five hundred I would do it.

I dialed home.

"Michael!" The Mayor said instantly. "How did it go?"

"The Witch-Queen said she'd discuss it over dinner."

"No way! Dinner Roulette?" Kyle's voice came from the background.

"Yes, and I'm sure nowhere near as many people have died as you—"

"WHAT?" Grandma Peterson yelled.

"I'M GOING TO EAT WITH HER!" I shouted into the phone.

"WHY?"

"BECAUSE SHE WANTS TO TALK TO ME!"

Someone wrestled the phone from her. "Tonight?" Grandpa Franklin said.

"No, in ten days," I said.

"Do you need more money?" he asked, with the slightest hesitation.

The village had pooled funds to get me here, and pay for my room in the cheapest hotel they could find. Would I just have to live on the streets for a few days?

Ten days of unwashed man would sure make a great second impression at a fancy restaurant.

"Hold up," Grandpa Franklin said. "Your mom just asked if they gave you a number to call."

"Let me check." What if they spent all the rest of their money and it didn't pan out? Of course, if this didn't pan out... I looked over the card and saw a number on it. "There is a number. Let me call them real quick."

"Sure," Grandpa said. "Bye!"

"Bye for now." I hung up, then immediately dialed the number.

The voice was female and British, but thankfully not the Witch-Queen. "Magister Alice Stephenson speaking, who is this?"

"Um, my name is Michael Mason, and—"

"What do you need?"

"I need somewhere to stay."

A pause, and muttering in Latin. "We may have to move you to another hotel. We'll contact you again. Do you need a stipend?"

"Uh... No, no, I think I'll be fine."

"Are you sure? You might have looked at the prices in stores here."

I hated to beg for anything else—but she was right. What if I needed something? "Sure. I mean, yes, uh, a stipend would be nice."

"It'll be in your account tomorrow. Anything else?"

"I think I'm good."

"Very good. Farewell." She hung up.

I sat on my bed, utterly disoriented.

The Capital had a place of worship, usually several, for every religion, sect, and cult in the world. The Basilica of St. Albert Magnus was the largest church in the world, let alone the largest Catholic church. Rumor had it the Witch-Queen made it personally with her construction daemons, as a gift to Pope Augustine II for surrendering to her.

Whatever the case was, the day after the audience, I didn't want to be in a crowd, just alone with God. And the streets of the Capital were very much crowded, all foot traffic except for the gondoliers and the airborne carriages above. As I struggled to navigate the streets and not get pushed into a canal, I spotted an ornate church along the way. *St. Malachi Catholic Church*, read the inscription above the front door.

I hurried inside. As I dipped my fingers in the brass holy water font to bless myself, I relaxed. *This* was normal. It looked like any other Catholic church, down to the colorful mess of posters and plastic rosaries in bags tacked to the wall.

There was a sign with a universal *no* over a spirogram: USE OF DAEMONS PROHIBITED INSIDE. *That* was different than home, but probably necessary for the Capital.

I stepped inside into the nave, which was still crowded, but probably less so than the Basilica would be. The incense wafted strongly in my nose. I walked up to the poor box and hesitated.

I was used to tithing, one of the few things Mom and Dad agreed on, but I had never tithed an amount so large. I would have written a check, but I couldn't physically write the number, so I just withdrew from the stipend in cash.

I looked around to make sure no one was looking, then stuffed 1000 IM down the slot.

I breathed deeply, and tried not to think about the money.

I went to the altar rail before the sanctuary, and knelt.

No, if I prostrated myself before the ruler of the world, I had to do more for God. I lay flat on the ground.

"Are you all right?" a voice whispered.

I looked up to see an old priest in a cassock looking down at me with concern. "I'm... doing... not so well," I admitted.

"If you want to talk, we can talk in the sacristy."

"I'd appreciate it." I got up, brushed myself off, and followed him through a door to the side.

"I am Father Jeffrey Xavier," he said. "What's on your mind?"

"This is going to sound crazy, but the Witch-Queen invited me for dinner."

"And you're afraid because...?"

"Because I might get poisoned," I said sheepishly. "I know it's unlikely..."

"Quite. More people have died by falling into the canals than have been casualties to assassination attempts. Yet I don't suppose you worry about the former as you walk around the Capital."

"I actually *did*—I, er, am new here. I'm actually from the North American Southeast Dominion. Maybe I should start at the beginning."

"That would help," Fr. Xavier replied with an amused smile.

I explained it as much as I could.

He nodded thoughtfully. "Think of it this way. If it is God's will that you really do die, you can intercede for your village from Heaven. Or perhaps the Witch-Queen will grant your petition in your memory."

"I guess," I said, not comforted.

"Or perhaps you are just afraid of her not granting your petition and it's coming out as fear of death?"

I sighed.

"We all experience events out of our control. We can only pray for God's mercy, and the strength to endure if he lovingly allows evil to occur."

"Right. I am still a little afraid."

"When is this dinner, if I may ask?"

"Nine days from now."

"I'll get you a novena to St. Louis IX. You take those nine days and pray and prepare your soul. You might still fall into a canal tomorrow, after all. Then forget about it. Worrying about the future won't make it any easier."

"Yes, sir." And now I did feel a little relieved.

Nine days later, I took an aerial cab, which was sweet, but I could barely focus on the ride.

Even in Lumberton I had heard of the Needle's Eye: a gourmet restaurant suspended by daemonic power over a tall, thin tower, with a kitchen for every kind of food in the world. The prices, I was sure, were even sky-higher.

So I walked in the front door and pretended I had any damn clue what I was supposed to do. The maître d' nodded at my presence as if recognizing me by sight. "Michael Mason, sir?"

"Yes, sir."

I could see him using all of his butler powers not to smile that I had called *him* sir. "Right this way, sir," he said, and I followed him to an elevator.

Calm down, I told myself, and breathed deeply. As the elevator rapidly ascended I said a prayer under my breath. Then we left the tower behind and were suspended in thin air. All around I saw the sprawling Capital, the Mediterranean in the distance, the colossal Palace nearby.

Then we were back inside a building. The maître d' had not even flinched. "This way, sir."

In the wide room that swayed ever so slightly, diners chattered, drinking from wineglasses and eating luxurious-smelling dishes. I spotted many magisters in men's and women's evening wear—*way* more expensive than mine. I had never had one of those nightmares where you're naked in front of a crowd, but I felt like I was in one now. A band—human, not daemonic—played jazz on a stage. Wait staff zipped from table to table, carrying platters, while others waited beside tables for the slightest order.

"Sir, this way." I stopped gawking and followed the maître d'.

The Witch-Queen waited at a table by the window. I tried to brace myself for impact, but she was even more stunning up close. Really thin, too, which normally wasn't my type—*what the hell brain I don't even have anything in the same galaxy as a chance*—but she pulled it off well. She still wore a black dress with white gloves, but this one was more of an evening gown that perfectly filled out her shape. Around her neck hung a diamond pendant in the shape of a crescent moon, dangling gently over her small bosom. She wore the Imperial

Diadem and had plenty more diamonds in her hair, not to mention bracelets, earrings, and rings, but her smile outshone them all.

I stopped short and couldn't help but stare.

She raised an eyebrow. My ears burned. "Perfect, you're right on time," she said.

"Of course, Your Imperial Majesty," I said quickly, lowering myself carefully into the chair across from her.

"Now what shall I have today?" she mused. A waiter presented her with a menu—only one. She laid it out on the table, and snapped her fingers. "*Daisu o kudasai.*" Dice appeared in her hands with a pop. "Let's find out!"

She rolled them onto the menu. Then frowned, and tipped a die over. "Perfect. We'll have the signature camel meat. I was hungry for that."

"Of course, ma'am," the waiter said. "For your wine?"

She ordered something in booze-speak. I had the courage to say, "I don't drink alcohol."

"Don't you Catholics drink real wine?" she asked, but not in a hostile tone. I had no idea how she knew I was Catholic, but then again I had probably been secretly investigated in the last ten days.

"Well... yes, but..." At this point I launched into an immediate explanation of essence versus accidents so awesome that St. Thomas Aquinas looked down from Heaven and gave a huge thumbs-up to me—or so I wished I would have, but I simply finished, "My family has a bad history... we have addictive personalities..."

She raised an eyebrow. "One drink won't kill you, and you'll never be able to afford another."

What if this was it? What if this would make the smallest influence on her decision? And I found it hard to say no to someone so... *her*. "I can handle one drink," I said at last.

"Perfect."

The waiter, unmoved by our discussion, bowed and departed. Another took his place.

The other guests at the other tables didn't look at me. They looked past me, in the same way you avoid looking at doggy doo-doo that someone didn't pick up. Heat began creeping up the back of my neck. Then again, *they* didn't have the ear of the Imperatrix Mundi herself. If only for the next hour or so.

She seemed to be staring off into space. This close I could hear her whispering something. Commands to her daemons? She looked to me. "A lot of people run screaming 'Daemon!' whenever they see something inexplicable. So why do you say your problem is a daemon?"

"We don't know what else it could be." I kept my words steady.

"So? Magister time is quite valuable. We can't send someone to investigate every incident."

That's what the local magisterium said. "We can't get anyone to even come to our village, and we don't have gravitational gear."

"I can arrange for someone with a gravity mapper to come, but if—" She stopped herself. "Even if there is a daemon, it might hide beyond the brane. You would need a magister to know for sure."

Progress. I smiled graciously. "Thank you, ma'am. Please send someone. We don't have any way of fixing it on our own."

A waiter arrived with the appetizer, whatever it was. Some kind of weird toast? He set a wine bottle on the table and began listing its... its booze-pedigree, or whatever you call it. The Witch-Queen sniffed the cork, whispered, and two wine glasses appeared in her hands. Then the waiter poured.

"Drink the whole thing," she instructed.

"Lord, thank you for this meal, and grant that it is not poisoned so we both can enjoy it safely," I prayed.

A man at a nearby table guffawed, and a few others tittered at me.

"Hey," I said loudly enough to spite them. "If you don't want to pray for the health and safety of our queen, that's on you."

No one replied. But I felt eyes on me, and found the Witch-Queen was smiling softly at me. "Good," she said at last. "Now drink."

I drank. Would it really be that bad if I died to save her from poisoning? I mean, sure, she had a horrible reputation, but in person she seemed normal (and gorgeous). Maybe I had spent too long listening to Kyle. I finished the glass, the burning in my throat almost muted by my stronger mix of emotions: fear and... excitement?

"Now the food."

I took a bite. An orchestra of tastes played in my mouth. My tongue announced its complete and undying loyalty to the Witch-Queen.

Even I had to admit she had this system of food tasting figured out. She looked into my eyes for a few seconds—to see if I was losing consciousness, I supposed. I met those alert eyes and felt an almost tingling sense. "*Iitadekimasu,*" she said at last, with a snap of her fingers. Invisible hands lifted the plate and her glass to her. Utensils appeared in the air and fed her.

The whole daemonically-enhanced eating thing was just too weird, but if I concentrated on my own food I didn't have to look at her. Of course, it was hard *not* to look at her. This would have been the date of my dreams if it wasn't for circumstances.

What was I doing? This was my only chance to convince her. I met her eyes again and she raised an eyebrow. "Ma'am," I said. "We're running out of clean water."

"Really?" she asked. "Your petition said this problem started six months ago."

So she had read it! But what was the dinner for, then? "Ma'am, please understand, we are trying our hardest, but it keeps getting worse."

"Worse?"

"Just one well went bad at first. Then more. The daemon seems to have been corrupting the whole aquifer—"

"Who told you it was a daemon?" the Witch-Queen asked, suddenly angry.

"Er, no one, we just thought—"

"*Who told you* it was a daemon?"

"We just guessed!"

"Who guessed?"

"The Elders!"

"Do any of them have daemonological backgrounds?"

"Not to my—Grandma Peterson tried for a magister license when she was young, but she couldn't get a sponsor."

"Ah, yes, the corruption of the Old Magisterium." The Witch-Queen smiled, the wrath gone in an instant. "And what exactly do you want me to do?"

"Remove the daemon," I said.

"That's it?"

"That's it, ma'am."

The waiter arrived with the main course. Camel meat tasted like beef, believe it or not. He brought so much of it that even minus my share, the Witch-Queen had plenty to eat. And eat she did—she was a slender woman, but she ate like a lumberjack.

Or more, because I was already stuffed and my stomach was unsettled.

For a time she was silent but for whispers. I had a good enough sense of hearing to tell they were names. "Daniel Woolworth. Sean King. Kerry Johnson."

"Ma'am, we've had to buy water from outside," I ventured. "The well water seems safe enough to shower in, but you know how much water a village needs to drink—"

"Three thousand liters a day?"

I was dumbfounded. "Well, yes. Around that amount. We drive over and fill tanks."

She didn't speak for a while, eating the meat. The next course arrived. She looked at me expectantly. I looked at the food. It looked delicious, but my stomach was warning me that a single bite more...

"I'm sorry, ma'am. I can't eat another bite."

The entire restaurant froze. The jazz musicians almost missed a note. The wait staff looked on with horror.

The Witch-Queen raised an eyebrow, then smiled. "Really?"

"I'm really sorry, but I'm just full."

"I'm not."

"I'm sorry about that, but I am," I said, my voice getting louder.

She raised her voice, too. "You'll never eat out like this again."

"Thank you. I appreciate it. I'm full."

She leaned in. "You'll enjoy more."

"I won't, sincerely," I said, not leaning away.

"Try it. Vomit if you have to."

"I don't want to waste food."

She waved her hand. "Oh, hush. It's my gift."

"Can't I taste just a bite?"

"Sure, if you keep eating after that."

"Can't you find someone else?"

"What? You don't find my company enchanting?" she said with quirked lips.

"I do," I insisted. "I would find it even more enchanting if I could stop eating."

"What if I enchanted you so you *couldn't* stop eating?"

"What the hell would that be, the Yuno Gasai approach to dinner dates?"

She froze for a moment. So did I. What had I done? Shocked understanding covered her face.

Then she bent over laughing.

My ears turned read as she laughed hysterically. She laughed so hard that she cried. The other guests looked on with confusion, but she kept laughing and laughing and laughing.

She sat up, giggled, and wiped her eyes. "You are the first person in the world to call me a *yandere*."

"You got the reference?" I asked, between wonder and horror. Yuno Gasai was the psycho girlfriend par excellence in the classic TV show *Mirai Nikki*, one of the best of an old genre of animation called anime. I had thought I was the only person who had even heard of it.

But apparently, so had she. "How did you even—"

"Old Blu-Rays at my village," I said. "And after the copyright reform..."

"Yeah, it's all legal," she said. "Shame they stopped making it. I always wondered if I should just subsidize the arts, there—" Then, as if she realized she was in public, she cleared her throat and turned to the waiter. "We are finished. But do bring the dessert."

I breathed a sigh of relief, as did my stomach.

"This alleged daemon. What does it do to the water?"

I was surprised at the pang of disappointment from the switch to a more 'normal' subject. Even her voice had changed from casual to imperial. "Makes it horribly brackish," I said, a little disoriented. "It's poisoned several people. We find usually boiling it makes it better, but..." I trailed off as she cocked her head at 'boiling.' "But we're never sure if it's safe after that."

"Why do you think boiling helps?"

"It just does."

"So how do you know it's a daemon?"

Something snapped in me. I slammed the table with my fist, rattling the dishes. "For God's sake, I don't know!" I shouted in frustration. "All I know is that our village is going to die of thirst unless you help. Please, *please*, just help us out!"

Silence fell around the room.

The Witch-Queen was unmoved. "Do you know how many magisters I've lost to traps that look just like this?"

I didn't know how to answer that.

"It's a pretty simple trick. You send a report that there's some 'wild' daemon out there, which is actually an anti-personnel Rank IV. My magister comes too close, and now there's one more bloody corpse on the road to counter-revolution."

"I—I'm sorry."

"And you? I think *you* are telling the truth, or at least you're so completely fooled that you think you're telling the truth. The question is, which one is it?"

I didn't know how to answer that.

"I insist on the dessert. You'll never have a like one again."

The wait staff came by with a plate of candied mushrooms, probably as delicious as the price tag had to be high.

Please, God, just calm my stomach. I opened my mouth, then stopped.

I motioned to the waitress. "What is this?"

"Candied cardamom mushrooms with dulche de leche, sir," she said.

I examined the dessert carefully, then spotted the gills. My whole body chilled. I looked to the Witch-Queen. "Ma'am, would you lean in?"

She looked confused, but did so.

"These aren't porcini. They're *Cortinarius orellannus*, the Fool's Webcap. Very deadly."

Her eyes bulged, but she said nothing, sitting back in her seat. Then she motioned to her waiter, and whispered something in his ear. He bowed and hurried off. She began whispering in Japanese, snapping her fingers now and then. "Act natural," she said calmly.

"I will," I said, unable to take my eyes from the deadly dessert.

In a few moments, which dragged on and on as the Witch-Queen just sat there, the chef arrived and genuflected. "What can I do for you, Your Imperial Majesty?"

"What is this?" the Witch-Queen asked icily.

"Candied cardamom mushrooms with dulche de leche, one of our specialties."

"*What* mushrooms?"

"Porcini, ma'am. A prized ingredient."

"You wouldn't mind having some yourself?"

He looked insulted, but not afraid. "As Her Imperial Majesty wishes." He reached for one.

I grabbed his wrist. "Stop!"

The Witch-Queen glared.

"These aren't porcini."

He looked even more offended. "What do you mean?"

"I can identify mushrooms, and these are the Fool's Webcap."

I had thought 'white as a sheet' was just an expression. He stared at them with terror and his mouth gaped wide. "I... er, well, I...didn't..."

"Convenient, isn't it?" The Witch-Queen raised her voice. "The one mushroom you serve just *happens* to have a dangerous look-alike."

I used all my courage to interrupt her. "Porcini really are one of the most prized culinary mushrooms. All sorts of fancy restaurants sell them."

"Yes! Yes!" the chef protested. "I had no idea!"

The Witch-Queen glared at me again.

"He was about to eat it without hesitation. You don't eat your own poison without at least thinking about it for a moment."

She glanced between us, then relaxed. "Where did you get these?"

"They were just with the rest of the ingredients. I don't know their source off-hand!" the man pleaded.

The Witch-Queen stood. "Attention!"

Everyone and everything stopped.

"Someone has attempted to poison me. No one is leaving until we've searched the premises and questioned all guests and staff. The assassin may or may not be here. Remain calm. We can all make it out of here alive. And don't eat the mushrooms!"

A noblewoman looked queasy, then vomited on the floor.

The Witch-Queen sat down again. "This is going to take a while, and I will be very busy. But rest assured, I will send someone to your village."

I felt elated, both that we were saved and because I felt I've-impressed-the-girl on an entire doping scandal's worth of steroids. I bowed my head. "Thank you so much, Your Imperial Majesty."

Magisters appeared with a whoosh. She got up without another word and went to them. I sat back, then decided to get some seltzer water at the bar to steady my stomach.

It was hours before I got to go back to the hotel. The Special Magical Police talked to me for what felt like an hour alone, although maybe the Witch-Queen had told them to be gentle. After all, if I hadn't been on her side I could have just said nothing and let her kidneys be destroyed. I would have probably died, too, but what was one more corpse on the way to counter-revolution?

When I did get back, I fell on the bed and instantly fell asleep.

The food had been delicious. The stomach upset the next morning was not. I spent a good deal of time puking into the toilet. I wondered if I'd actually eaten some other poison, but concluded it was probably the camel meat or some spice that disagreed with me, since my stomach wasn't accustomed to such rich food.

Offerings to the porcelain god complete, I stumbled back to the living room of my suite and turned on the TV. Nothing but the Witch-Queen, the Eye of the Needle, and me. Figured. I wished they had another picture of me than a brief screenshot from my petition—but what, did I *want* fame?

Nah. The important thing? Mission accomplished. A strange part of me deeply wished I could see the Witch-Queen again, though. She had been known to level rebelling cities, but for a brief moment she just seemed like a cute young weeb.

I had heard her called the Antichrist, what with her ID cards to participate in commerce and her new calendar. The fact that the Pope had surrendered to her was proof to some Protestants that she was indeed the Antichrist, approved by the second beast. It was proof to some Catholics that the Pope had renounced the throne of St. Peter and now there was no Pope. The Orthodox were pretty chill overall once she had returned the Hagia Sophia. But now whatever anyone thought, none dared say a word against her louder than a whisper.

But whoever she was, hadn't she made the world a *little* better? My best friend could recite every last misdemeanor of her crimes, but maybe she was just misunderstood?

"Breaking update from the Palace." The news anchor switched to a pretty young lady—though now that I had met the Witch-Queen, all lesser girls seemed nowhere near as pretty. "The Special Magical Police has released a statement saying they believe the poisoning incident was an accident. They are currently continuing to investigate how the deadly mushrooms entered the supply chain..."

Huh, the one time where they nearly get her is the time they weren't even trying. Crazy world.

My phone rang—all nines, notoriously always the Witch-Queen's caller ID. I froze. But...didn't I *want* to see her again?

I tapped the answer button.

"Hey! Is this Michael Mason?"

"Yes, Your Imperial Majesty."

"I'm right outside your door," she said casually. "Let me in!"

"I'll open it!" I hurried out and found the Imperatrix herself, hand with pinky and thumb extended like a phone against her face.

"Perfect!" she said, and flipped her hand to "hang up." She marched past me into the hotel room.

I realized, to my regret, that the place was a mess, and the bathroom still smelled of vomit. Thankfully, that was the only thing that smelled of vomit. She hopped onto my bed without a care in the world.

What on Earth? She had seemed so formal last night.

"So!" she said cheerfully. "I've decided to change policy, because of you. No more leaving these things uninvestigated."

"The poisoning?" I asked.

"No. The only policy I'm changing there is no more mushrooms." She paused, and in that one moment I saw a deep loneliness flicker through her eyes. "I'm talking about your village."

"What?" I asked.

"Let me tell you a daemonological fact: free daemons do not interfere with the material brane. It was a daemon, and it was not 'wild.'" She sighed, and her shoulders slumped ever so slightly in overwhelming weariness. "We'll have to investigate every last one of these from now on. If you hadn't told me, it would have tainted the whole water table."

"You're welcome," I said, blushing.

"Yes. I am welcome," she said with a mischievous gleam. "But I haven't thanked you yet, have I?"

"Uh..."

"We'll have to make a good show of it, in the end. I can't be arbitrary, only whimsical. The Witch-Queen has to be selfish, too, you know," she said to herself. "Anyone I ever show care about just becomes another target. Everything has to ultimately be about me. So I've decided to grant you a position that will make *all* of us happy."

"What?" I pleaded.

"Chief Anime Watching Buddy to the Crown."

2

COMPANION TO THE CROWN

There was a silence in the hotel room lasting half an hour, or at least that's what it felt like. The Witch-Queen smiled brightly, and I just stood there.

"Chief Anime Watching Buddy," I repeated.

"Yeah. I bet you don't know anyone else who watches it, do you? *I* sure don't."

The Witch-Queen looked gleefully serious. I couldn't say I didn't like the idea of watching it together, especially with someone as cute as her—not that I had the chance the size of an microbe. But how I could provide for my mom? "I'm sorry, ma'am," I said. "My family is very, very poor, and I need to get back to Lumberton so I can work—"

"Nonsense," she said with a smile. "Money is never an issue with me."

I supposed it wasn't. "How long do you want me to do this?" I asked, head spinning.

"Oh, I don't know. I'm told my moods are mercurial. But you'll make bank."

I opened my mouth to argue, then closed it again. I mean, sure, we could use the money, but I couldn't just stay here... but c'mon, wasn't this going to be the only time an opportunity like this would pop up? Not the money, but watching anime with, of all people, the Witch-Queen. "I could do it for a time," I found myself saying.

"Perfect! Alice will get the formalities sorted, then we can watch. We'll put on a great appearance. I need more screaming cartoon people in my life." She tilted her head. "Oh, snap! Got a meeting pending. See you!" Without another word, she bounced off the bed and skipped out.

I stood there in silence, staring at the dent she had left in the mattress. What had just happened?

Alice arrived little more than an hour later, turning out to be a tall woman in a magister's suit with a long black cape. "Magister Alice Stephenson, D.A.D.," she said. "We talked earlier on the phone. May I come in?"

I wondered if that was the sort of thing you shouldn't give a magister a positive answer to. Daemonology had existed for eighty years, but like most people I knew nothing more than rumors. Would inviting her in give her daemons permission? "Sure," I said anyway.

She muttered something as she stepped in, and invisible hands closed and locked the door behind her with a click. We walked back into the living room of my suite. "I'm the manager for the Imperial Household," she said. "I'm more or less the Imperatrix's mom."

My brain did not process this information. "What?"

"I wouldn't call her immature. Just that with her life, she drops balls. Lots of them. And you can't bind a daemon to fix everything."

"Oh."

"If you're wondering, she found out what I was calling myself, and she found it hysterical."

"Her Imperial Majesty seems to take jokes well."

"She does," Alice agreed, then looked serious. "Thank you for saving her."

"Not a problem."

"You'll officially be an employee of the Imperial Palace. Sometimes..." She stopped. "Sometimes Lynn can just use a friend."

"Lynn?"

"Her Imperial Majesty Lynn. You might have heard of her." Her lips had an ironic turn, not unlike the Witch-Queen herself.

"No, I mean... you're on a first name basis with her?" I asked.

"Some of her closest associates are. I would be cautious about using her name unless she tells you do so. She can be... easily upset."

Was it just yesterday that the Imperatrix had almost ordered a chef to commit accidental suicide via dessert? Yet she didn't seem that upset at anything else I said or did.

"Speaking of being cautious, be very careful not to repeat anything she tells to you anyone else. Not your mom, not your best friend, not your priest, not even anyone on the staff or in the Imperial Court. If you leak something sensitive and she is harmed, well, inadvertent treason is still treason."

"I see." Maybe I didn't actually want this job after all. But then again, anime with *her*...

"The good news is that you'll be very well compensated. Just to give an example of what she can do, one of—one of the staff members had a sister with a rare form of cancer. Lynn ordered a research team to develop a drug for it. She enjoys granting favors, as long your request isn't outrageous. And maybe even then."

"Huh."

"By the way, don't ask for a noble title or a change in Imperial policy. The former will inevitably make you miserable. The later *will* make her upset."

"I understand." I didn't even want a title to begin with.

"And now for the paperwork." She said something in Latin and a suitcase appeared with a pop. She opened it to show two stacks of papers that completely filled the interior. "This is about a third of it. Most of it is just stuff to read later—forms of etiquette, a guide to the Palace, and a directory of important officials. You won't need the last one unless you offend someone, which I suggest you don't. But please, take your time reading over the contracts." She handed me a thick sheet of paper and a pen. "I'll be back in an hour." She got up, spoke in Latin, and disappeared.

That sounded less promising than a series of statements about the future prepared by a lawyer. I looked at the pages and realized that this was worse: *nobles* had prepared this.

Six years ago, the world was obsessed with individual consent and personal liberty. When the Witch-Queen came with her legions of daemons to start a revolution, many revolted with her. When the last of the nations fell, the world had replaced freedom with an obsession with Imperial fiat and appeasing the powerful. The paperwork was less about ensuring my free choice in the matter and more about agreeing that I did or did not fit into an endless number of categories of good and bad established by contradictory Imperial Edicts, as well as smaller if no less byzantine local decrees. Lumberton was so far into the countryside that we were shielded from most of this nonsense, but every time we drove out a truck of lumber there was some new hoop to jump through.

I wasn't in Lumberton anymore.

Still, I thought, as I began the process by swearing via solemn affidavit I was not engaged in the business of slaughtering of animals for fur (unless I was also eating the meat or the animal was a pest animal under I.E. 14455 subsection 5(c), provided that...), *still*, why not? This was going to be the easiest job in the world, right? Just watch anime to keep a cute girl happy. Sure, she was the Imperatrix Mundi, but as long as I kept my head on straight, figuratively, I would keep my head on literally.

After agreeing I would not use values in the metric system that were exactly equal to old customary units, unless I.E. 2041 or I.E. 1025 applied, I reached the consent form for an indefinite change of jurisdiction.

Officially, immigration between dominions was limited to keep their cultures intact and their sizes equal and "fair." In practice, it kept people under the thumbs of their local rulers. Though the form needed my permission, it also needed the permission of the King of Atlanta and the Viceroy of the Capital.

I looked the form all over and could not see any date on it. Oh well. I agreed I was not attempting to flee from a felony unless I also fell under one the amnesty edicts or an Imperial Pardon.

Then, finally, the actual employment contract. It was just three pages, front and back. I was relieved, then stared at the numbers.

I would be paid 20,000 IM a week, with a sign-on bonus of 200,000 IM.

I counted the zeros, but nope. I would be making more in a week than I did in an entire year as a lumberjack. The Witch-Queen hadn't been kidding.

I sat back and held my head.

What would I do with the money? What *could* I do with it? The number was too big to think about. I was sure a noble wouldn't hesitate to use the same amount as toilet paper (I.E. 1457 be damned) but...

No, duh, I'd just send it home. I only needed a little, after all. Satisfied, I flipped through the remaining pages, and signed my name.

On cue, the doorbell rang. I opened it to find Alice. "Done with most of it?" she asked.

"I got one stack done."

She sighed. "Did you try to read the paperwork?"

"Yes. So?"

"About once a month when we get a new staff member, Lynn has to pardon them of some obscure edict. As long as you're on her good side, laws aren't that important."

"I want to know what I'm signing. I'm promising something with my own name."

"Good for you. You'll be spending several more hours, then, but you can finish it up tonight Anyway, this is yours, once we get your account set up." She handed me a small card covered with daemonic spirograms.

I nearly dropped it.

Only Grandma Peterson, the oldest Elder of Lumberton, could remember the time before daemonic hacking, when anyone could get a debit card. Now the system was only for the rich, those who could afford to have a daemon bound to their card to protect it.

A category I would soon apparently belong to.

"If you lose this, I can track it down, but it will be a huge hassle," she said. "By the way, there is technically a credit limit on this, but if it gets in the way just give the number on the back a call."

"This is a *credit* card?" I asked.

"Yes. Like I said, there is a limit. Just don't go to an auction house unless she brings you."

I took a deep breath. This was going to my new normal, wasn't it? At least until Her Imperial Majesty got bored of anime. Or me. "All right."

"Now we have to set you up with an account at the Imperial Bank. I don't think your local credit union has a branch here, unfortunately." Another ironic smile.

"I don't think so either," I said. "Ready when you are."

"Do you have anything you need to pack first?"

"Uh..."

"You'll get an apartment in the Palace complex. It will save you time getting through security."

"All right," I said. "I haven't unpacked since they moved me here. Let me go get it."

"I'll arrange that. We should get moving."

As we left my suite for the last time, I realized in my nine days there it had given me at least a slight sense of security. Now I had zero idea what the hell was happening.

Something nagged at me as I followed her to a waiting cab. I mean, sure, this was kinda nuts for just being an anime watching buddy... but it was the Witch-Queen. But why would Alice suggest Her Imperial Majesty might take me to an *auction house*?

I was still wondering as I passed through Palace security, in one of the several gatehouses surrounding the border of the complex. This one was for nobles, but then Alice cut me through to the front of the VIP line. I felt the envious eyes of a hundred sharks reduced to minnows.

The Palace was not the tallest building in the world, but it was up there. The black dome where the Witch-Queen herself lived was supported by three long, thick "bridges" where gravity was turned at a right angle. Below that was a colossal base structure, where the Imperial government sat. In between, in the middle of the bridges, was a giant enclosed disc with no windows, which rumor had it held massive summoning circles for powerful daemons.

Trolleys moved around on rails in the courtyard. Above, magisters flew, hazy outlines surrounding them. Alice flagged down a trolley and we hopped on to get to one of the multiple apartment buildings.

We stopped at the fanciest-looking one, or was that just my imagination? Alice handed me a keycard, also covered with daemonic inscriptions. "Just take the rest of the day off. The ceremony will be Monday."

The ceremony? I was too tired to think. "Thanks."

A minute later, I entered my new apartment and found it already furnished in a retro-20s style. Good thing I liked it, because I definitely couldn't afford to change the decor.

No, wait, I *could.*

What the hell? It still didn't register.

Whatever. I wasn't going to be Mr. Man-Diva about it. Besides, it looked cool. Fitting, if we were going to be watching stuff from the previous century.

I sank into the immaculate recliner, and relaxed a little. So the Witch-Queen wanted a friend. I could be one. Why not enjoy whatever little time I had with her? Plus, I didn't think it was my imagination that I had seen those moments of loneliness. It wouldn't hurt to make her feel a little less lonely. I would do the same for anyone.

I got out my wallet and tried to fit all my new cards in. I glanced at my new ID, and felt a strange sense of loss. Almost five years ago, I had exchanged my driver's license and social security card for my old ID, wondering how long the

Witch-Queen's reign would actually last. And now... I knew her personally. Sorta.

How much longer would I know her?

I looked around. "This is temporary," I reassured myself. "We're just going to have this until she gets bored. It won't last."

The decor didn't answer me. I should probably see how many rooms this place had, come to think of it. Once I was ready to comprehend more (temporary) wealth, that is.

I also should really tell Mom. But what could I tell her? I didn't know if I could even tell her about the anime. But I had to tell her something.

`Hey, Mom! I don't know what I can talk about just yet, but I got a temporary job at the Capital. It`

I stopped myself. Could I say how much it paid?

`It pays well. Don't tell anyone yet. Dunno when I can come back. Love.`

I pressed send.

Texts were often laggy in the Capital for some reason, so I didn't expect a quick response. I opened the suitcase and fished out the handbook for employees, flipping to a random page.

> *Under no circumstances are you to initiate physical contact with Her Imperial Majesty. Doing so may lead to your immediate termination as well as further charges under I.E. 73...*

Wait, I.E. 73? Edicts were numbered in the order she issued them, starting from her self-declaration of world rulership. This had to be within her first few months of power. Had she been touched inappropriately? Had there been an attempted assassination? Or was she just not a touchy-feely person?

I set down the book. Mysteries could wait, too. I was hungry, but I had a sinking feeling that if I called Alice I would end up with a private chef. And that would be a line I wouldn't cross.

"That's my line," I said out loud. "She can give me as much money as she wants, but I'm not going to have servants. No one waiting on me hand and foot. I'm just an ordinary person."

The decor once again was silent, as if passive-aggressively reminding me it was much better than what I had at home.

My phone dinged.

`Money isn't important, you are. Be careful.`

`I will, Mom`

I slipped the envelope into the poor box after Mass. There. Money wasn't important.

But why were my hands shaking?

As I stepped out into the sunshine, my phone rang: Grandpa Franklin. I hurried to the shade of the building.

"Did they come?" I asked.

"Yes! It was amazing! We were miles away and we could hear the battle. The ground kept shaking and shaking. Then it was over."

"Was anyone hurt?"

"No, but we lost a few houses. It's nothing compared to having water again!"

I breathed a sign of relief. At least, whatever was going to happen, the Witch-Queen had saved us.

"The SMP talked to a few of us afterwards. Not me, but they got Grandma Peterson going. They were asking us about where the daemon came from."

I could imagine. "She told me it wasn't wild."

"She?"

"The Witch-Queen," I said sheepishly.

There was dead silence on the other end for a few seconds.

"Hello?" I asked. "Still there?"

"I'm here. That's... what they said. They wanted to make sure none of us had summoned it, I think." Another pause. "You coming back today?"

How on Earth could I describe what had happened? "Um, just watch TV tomorrow, INN. It'll be easier than me explaining."

"Be careful."

"I will."

The ceremony was so solemn it had to be the Witch-Queen's elaborate self-satire. The two of us were at her dais, and her highest-ranking ministers and magisters, including Alice Stephenson, stood at attention in her other-wise-empty throne room. Several news crews watched in the background.

"This commoner has both saved my life and discovered a new threat to the Empire," the Witch-Queen said. "If any of you watching at home suspect daemonic activity, dial the number you see on screen. Meanwhile, I will reward the competent."

My ears felt hot, but I didn't look behind me, as I was kneeling on the dais. For once, I wished I had followed politics more. I knew some people were obsessed with the Imperial Court, but what did I know?

"Well?" the Witch-Queen asked me.

"I hereby swear to be a good friend and companion..." I swore. I was always leery of swearing oaths, but technically this was an official position, so I guess it was fine. At least it was short.

She looked as serious as a heart attack. I tried my absolute hardest to keep a straight face. "Arise, my new Companion," she said, and handed me my cere-monial sword.

It was a katana.

She had a closed reception afterwards. No reporters, no guards, no one but the Witch-Queen, her government, and myself. The room was way too big for us, but the acoustics were weird—there was no echo of our soft voices.

Buffet tables stood along the side, and a few other small tables were scattered in the center with chairs, but no one seemed particularly enthusiastic about the food.

Just about everyone talked to me. Introductions, congratulations and what I took to be desultory attempts at schmoozing. I guessed even the Chief Anime Watching Buddy was a rank of power. Better that than dog doo-doo, at any rate.

"I am Darius Janus, Imperial Minister of Daemonology," one gaunt, balding man introduced himself. I recognized his sharp features and expression from TV and magazines: he had been one of the most prominent magisters in the world before the Witch-Queen took over, and had in fact had led the Old Magisterium's attempt to stop her. She had subsequently decided—for whatever inexplicable reason—not only to spare him, but to give him a high position.

Like I had room to talk about inexplicable reasons. "Pleased to meet you, Magister Janus."

"I'm curious about this daemon you discovered in your village. Perhaps some time we could talk about it?"

"I don't know much, to be perfectly honest. Was it an anti-personnel Rank IV?"

He raised an eyebrow. "Not anti-personnel, but it was a Rank IV, strangely enough."

"Time to eat!" the Witch-Queen announced, and the room formed an unhappy line in front of the tables. I found myself ahead of her, and the line slowly moved ahead. Floating utensils passed out the food. The magisters had hovering plates. The non-magisters carried hefty trays.

"Got to be careful with the buffet," the Witch-Queen told me. "People find the most elaborate ways of spiking the punch. And not with alcohol, if you know what I mean."

"Why do you even have it, then?"

"Anyone who poisons us has to poison *all* of us. Cuts down on the would-be traitors."

I understood at that moment why everyone was deathly unenthusiastic yet got one of everything.

We sat at a table. "So," she said. "What kind do you like?"

It took me a moment to figure out what she was referring to. "Mecha, mostly. Though I'll watch anything!" I hastily added.

"Good. I liked *Escaflowne*, and I've heard *RahXephon* was good, but I never watched the latter."

"I've seen, like, three episodes of *RahXephon*."

"Really? Why? Is it not that good?"

"I don't know. I liked it, but the library only had the first disc, and our internet connection is too bad to stream."

"Huh," the Imperatrix said. She got out a cellphone—one of those daemon-proof smartphones. I had never imagined I would be within five feet of one. Of course, I never imagined I might be drinking the same potentially-poisoned punch as the Witch-Queen, either. She tapped away on the screen, and whispered in Japanese. "Found a copy. We'll watch it this Thursday."

"Sounds like a plan!" I said, feeling the usual disorientation around her. I wondered if I would get used to it.

I had half-expected her to have us watch in an empty movie theater, but it was actually just an ordinary room in the Palace. I did not, thankfully, have to wear my ceremonial katana.

She sat—perched, more like—on one of two grandly embroidered recliners in front of a massive flatscreen TV. She wore a black dress as usual, though a less fancy one than the one she wore to audiences. One white-gloved hand held a remote.

"Well, are you going to sit?" she asked with a smile. Her eyes looked into mine.

I was stunned for a moment by the intensity. "Um, of course, Your—"

"Oh, knock it off. Call me Lynn."

"Lynn." That was quick. She wanted a friend, after all. But why did she look at me with such interest in her eyes?

I sat on the other recliner. She pressed play.

RahXephon is an anime about a young man living in an alternate Tokyo, except singing aliens invade and he finds a giant god-robot, and... it's a complicated anime plot. But I felt suddenly more attracted to the story of a guy being yanked out of his world by a girl he doesn't know into another, stranger world.

We watched the whole thing, uninterrupted except by our occasional commentary. The only odd part, besides watching TV with the Witch-Queen, was that she still whispered names constantly. "Alexander Ariti. Ishigawa Jumpei. Kevin McPhearson."

"I'm liking this," she declared after the show was over. "It's been a while since I last watched. I forgot what Japanese sounded like a century ago."

"You speak Japanese?" We had watched it subbed. Wait, duh, you idiot, she's been commanding her daemons in Japanese this whole time...

Lynn didn't seem offended. "I speak twenty-eight languages," she said without pride. "I pick up a new one every now and then when I'm bored. But Japanese was my first." She looked at me, again with the same intense gaze. "What do you speak?"

"Oh, just English," I said, a little embarrassed at my lack of linguistic achievement. "I know bits and pieces of Japanese and Latin. I, uh, never went to college."

"Nor did I," she said with a wink. "Self-study and daemonic tutors for me. But I took classes after I conquered the world."

"Did you get a scholarship for that? The Imperial Grant for Young Empresses?" I said with a grin.

"Ha!" she said with a matching grin. "I had the best teachers in the world." Then she looked thoughtful. "What would you like to study?"

"I, uh, am happy being a lumberjack."

"Come on, there's probably something you've wanted to learn."

"I've thought about theology sometimes, but..."

"Perfect. You can start next week."

"Uh..."

"It's my present. You'll be bored a lot of the time when I'm busy. You can learn instead."

"Sounds like a plan," I said, unsure if it actually *did* sound like a plan.

She hopped up and walked to the door. "See you!"

"Wait!" I called.

She stopped with a raised eyebrow. "Yes?"

"Thanks for saving us, Your Imperial Majesty."

"You're welcome. And I told you, call me Lynn." And without another word, she was gone.

Sure enough, Alice showed up the next day with a stack of thick books. "You'll be studying with a professor named Alexander Jameson, starting next Friday."

"Wait, wait, wait, *who?*" I asked.

"Recognize the name?"

Of *course* I recognized the name. He was the world's foremost expert on the theology of daemons. He was even appointed to the original Gravitationally-Attracted Being Commission by Augustine I. He had to be over a hundred, now, but when the Witch-Queen came knocking... "He's famous in Catholic circles."

"Believe me, when she likes you, you get the best of the best."

Maybe being Lynn's friend, paid or not, had its perks. I glanced over the textbooks. I wouldn't waste this opportunity—this *gift.*

"If there's anything else you want, just ask," Alice said. "The world is always a little safer when she's happy."

"I hope."

"Don't just hope. Keep her happy." She bowed and headed out.

I sat down and opened up the book on top, but then my phone rang: Kyle Franklin. That was unusual. Kyle rarely called, because he was sure the "Imperials" had the phone system wiretapped. I was sure he was correct in this case, but what exactly could you do about it?

"Mike, you all right, man?" he asked, softly, as if a whisper could hide from the Witch-Queen's spying daemons.

"I'm fine, dude."

"She hasn't, er..."

"Hasn't what?"

"Well, you know the rumors and all."

Oh no. I was scared that for once I *didn't* know where this was going. "What rumors?"

"Her harems."

"Her harem?"

"No, harems, plural! She has three, after all."

"Listen, Kyle, oh my *God*—" Where did I even start? "Three?"

"Men, women, and daemons."

I shouldn't have asked. My free hand went to my face. "You need to spend a lot less time on the Internet—"

"No, no, she has information-censoring daemons that scrape the truth off the web."

"Then you need to spend *more* time on the Internet. For goodness' sake, doesn't she have better things to do than..."

"No! She doesn't! She spends all her time—"

"Kyle, please. I can't talk about it."

"Of course not. Her nefarious yet highly seductive magicks—"

"For God's sake, Kyle, she's a real human being, not an anime character!" I shouted. "Anyway, even if she was doing something awful, why the hell would I talk about it over the phone?"

"Just get out. While you still can." He hung up.

I sighed. Sure, Kyle was Kyle. But what did Lynn want, really?

What would I do if Lynn asked for something more than platonic friendship? If she did have a harem or three, she was going to pick people who would never talk.

But she was the Witch-Queen, after all. Who could tell her no?

Yet she didn't ask. We just talked.

"The thing is," Lynn said after one episode. "I get that the writers didn't know how these things really work, and that it's working for the story. But that's a perfectly terrible waste of a SC if I ever saw one."

"A SC?"

"Daemonology term. A supercombatant. If you have a giant invincible robot, you send it against the other giant invincible robots. Not against the chaff."

"But there are no other giant invincible robots."

"Details." She smiled. Maybe Alice was right. It seemed everything in the world was a little better if Lynn smiled.

And so we watched the entire series, one episode a weekday except Wednesdays. While I was not privy to her schedule, I knew even thirty minutes with her was more than the average duke would manage in a lifetime.

Which made it all the stranger, and dare I say *alarming* when we would just keep talking, for another thirty minutes, then another, then another, as the time would just fly by...

"Did you live your whole life in Lumberton?" she asked one time.

"Until now, yes. I mean, we drove down to Memphis a few times."

"Tight-knit community?"

"Very. I mean, officially we have a Lord Mayor, though we just call him the Mayor." He had been the elected mayor before the Witch-Queen ended all forms of democracy, and so he had managed to keep the title. Sort of. "The Elders practically run the place. We all call them Grandpa and Grandma so-and-so, but we're not all related."

"Any of your relatives?"

"Actually, my parents both moved in before I was born. They wanted... a quiet life." That, at least, was true.

"You talk with your parents much?"

"Hey, let's talk about something else." My voice rose with irritation.

"Sure thing," she said, then glanced at the clock. "Oh *crap* I had a meeting. Darn it." She sighed. "I'll..."

I looked at her, but she seemed totally lost in thought.

"Is it worth... no, no, I shouldn't," she muttered. "We'll have to skip tomorrow."

"That's all right," I said, hiding my disappointment. Still, what did right did I have to protest? It was just a game, and she was paying me to play...

"See you!" As she stepped outside, my heart told me the truth: I would still be playing, even without the money.

Mike, listen. I get that you want to help me, but I don't need all this money. There are other people who need it more.

Sorry, Mom.

There's no reason to be sorry. I'm just telling you I don't need it.

I had read the texts over and over again, until I worked up my courage to head to the Imperial Bank branch. "I want—I want to transfer money to St. Malachi's Catholic Church," I said.

"How much, sir?"

"Eighteen," I said.

"Eighteen?"

"Eighteen thousand imperial marks, I mean?"

"Sir, is that how much you wish to send?"

I flushed. "Yes. Yes it is."

The clerk, who appeared to be a magister, chanted in some language. A daemonic typewriter by her typed up a form. She passed it to me. "Please sign here."

I signed, then handed it back.

The typewriter typed up a receipt.

"Is there anything else you need?"

"No, that will be all."

I went to a couch in the lobby to update my checkbook. Then I glanced at the receipt and my jaw hit the floor.

I still had 202,000 IM in my account.

How? I had sent or given everything. How was that even possible?

I hurried back to the line, sweating as I waited for my turn. When a teller called me, I couldn't make eye contact. "I... I believe there's been a mistake," I said.

"Sir?"

"I don't think I should have this money," I said. "My checkbook—isn't balancing."

The teller said something in Latin and clicked her tongue. "We can provide you with a transaction list."

"Yes, thank you. I'm very sorry about this."

She put lined paper into the typewriter, and moments later handed me a fresh statement. I hurried back to my couch.

I saw it immediately: the Palace had refilled my account back to 200,000 IM on my last payday.

I took a deep breath.

What the *HELL?!*

No. No, this was Lynn's doing. She wanted to spoil me, probably. What did money matter to the Imperatrix Mundi?

But why? I was just her anime watching buddy, not her... boyfriend.

But did she see it that way?

I felt as if I had clipped through the floor like in a buggy video game, and the physics engine was dragging me down into the abyss.

Wasn't this just a game to her, after all? A pretend friend, because no one really liked her? The thing with all games was that no matter how much you enjoyed them, they would always grow stale in the end. Just because she was wealthy enough to play with people instead of pixels didn't change that.

I took another deep breath. My heart didn't slow down. But was she even acting as if I was only a game?

Or deep within my heart, was I acting as if she was only my employer?

After all, Lynn behaved more like a girlfriend than my previous two actual relationships. She neither ghosted me nor was verbally abusive. In fact, she would actually text me to apologize if she couldn't make our anime...dates?

A week later, emergencies aside, we finished *RahXephon*. "Did that make any sense to *you?*" she asked.

"I think it's supposed to be one of those cryptic artsy endings."

"Yeah." She fell silent, except for muttering names under her breath. At last she said, "Kinda wish it didn't have to end this way."

My heart fell, but hope, like a desperate coup, wrested control of my mouth. "You mean the series—"

"No, my anime-watching career," she sharply interrupted. "The moment you mentioned Yuno Gasai in the Needle's Eye, my court instantly became the most decadent haven of weeaboos. I can never enjoy it normally again. And then—" she cut herself off. "But at least this was fun."

My brain's loyalists reestablished control. Screw it. May as well lay my cards on the table. "Are you saying you want to be done with me?"

She looked into my eyes, intense as ever, as if wondering how brave I could be to say that to her face. She whispered a few more names in the following silence. "You know what? No. Let's watch another mecha."

"How about *Mobile Suit Gundam 00*? It's one of the best."

"Sure thing." And Lynn smiled.

Kyle called me again, a few weeks later. "When are you coming back?"

"I have no idea."

"What is she doing with you?"

"I can't tell you," I said. "I really can't."

"Is—is it about the protests in Chicago?"

"What?" I glanced at my complimentary copy of the *Imperial Times* on the coffee table. There were no mention of protests on the front page.

"It's about them, isn't she? If it's not the harems, she's spying—"

Why would she even bring it up? "I haven't even heard of them!"

"Tell her we're not making unreasonable requests, all right? You can do that, right?"

"Listen, we don't have that kind of relationship," I told him. "We're just..." What the hell *were* we?

"Dude, are you OK?" His voice was suddenly concerned.

"As good as I can be."

"Listen, if you need an extraction... I have contacts," he confided.

Even if he did, what the hell could he help me with? Did *I* even know what I needed help with? Did I have any clue about what my life even was any more? "I'm managing," I tried.

"Really? What are you doing?"

"Do you *really* want to know what we do?"

For once in his life, Kyle shut up. I heard the slightest intake of breath.

"Lynn and I just watch an episode of an anime, maybe two if we have time. And we talk. Right now we're watching *Mobile Suit Gundam 00.*"

Another dead silence. "You... you think you're on a first name basis?"

"We are. She ordered me to call her Lynn."

"And she didn't tell you her last name?"

"No, but—"

"Then she's just luring you in! Wake up, man! One day it's *Gundam*, the next day you'll wake up in her pleasure chambers and find yourself with nothing but—"

I hung up on him. Then I hurled the phone away. I heard a snap as it slammed against the wall.

I picked it up and considered throwing it again.

Up until that moment, I didn't imagine Kyle and I would ever have something to separate us. We had been inseparable growing up, after all. Kyle was the weird kid, an outcast despite being Grandpa Franklin's actual grandson, and me, who tried to befriend him. He even watched an episode or two of *Gundam* on my insistence, but said he couldn't stand listening to a foreign language.

He had *not* taken the piecemeal surrender of America well. He was too sickly to enlist, which probably saved his life. When the Old Magisterium fell, conventional armies hadn't been able to stop the Witch-Queen's daemonic legions. Had she used her SCs? It would be interesting to hear *her* perspective on it.

I sighed. Kyle was just being Kyle. He hadn't intended to step on the weak point of my heart. Because it was already full to capacity, and crowding out money, anime, and my home were Lynn's smile and those intense emerald eyes.

For her part, Lynn never made any advances. At first I was waiting for her to even bring up the subject, but it never happened. We never even touched. Still, once I caught her glancing at me mid-episode while she caught me glancing at her. She grinned mischievously, and I looked away.

Kyle's words had hit their mark though. I didn't know what her last name was. No one but she did. No one even knew where she was born, or how the hell she had managed to get up to the Moon and back.

You know, though, maybe he had a point. If I knew for certain this was just a game... then I could play along until she got bored. Because from where I was sitting—five feet from her—she didn't look bored in the least.

One day, we skipped anime in favor of the Judgment Games. An earl accused of embezzling public funds was trying to cross a rickety bridge suspended over a pool of green slime. Armed with only a pool noodle, he fought off attacks of hovering pool noodles on his way to the other side. But there were a lot of them and only one of him, so more often then not the bridge would twist and he would go *ploosh*.

The timer ticked down. Lynn watched and laughed along with me after every failure.

"Are these things rigged?" I asked.

"Nope. That would take all the fun out of it. Difficult, though."

"One minute left!" the MC announced.

The noble clambered up the ladder. The moment he stepped aboard, pool noodles immediately swooped down to attack. He knocked back several, then desperately tried to charge across.

He didn't make it.

"And that's all!"

"*NO!*" screamed the noble. The camera zoomed in on his desperate face.

Mom hadn't been comfortable with me watching the show, but honestly, after being stepped on by the nobles long enough, it was fun to watch *them* being stepped on in the most ridiculous of ways.

"Honestly thought he might have made it," Lynn mused, then looked at the clock. "I *have* to get to this meeting in an hour, so let's just talk for a bit, all right?"

"Lynn, if I could ask a personal question..." Oh no, why did those words have to leave my mouth?

She raised an eyebrow.

"What's your last name?"

"Like the Japanese Emperor, those of Imperial rank need no last name." She looked deep into my eyes, with even more intensity.

"No worries. Just curious."

"Why do you ask?"

"I was just curious—"

"Why do you ask?" If her eyes bored into me any further they'd be cutting through the recliner into the wall.

"My, er, friend was wondering if you had told me. That's all."

She seemed satisfied. "I won't. But I'll let you in on a little secret. 'Lynn' is what they called me growing up. But it wasn't my legal name."

Great, now I was *more* confused. "I've always been Michael Mason. My friends call me 'Mike.'"

"What? You wouldn't mind it if I gave you a title?"

"I don't think Lord Mike sounds right. But they did call me the Fungus Lord, once upon a time."

"Oh, yeah, I meant to tell you," Lynn said. "The SMP found out the truth: *someone* somewhere along the line decided that he liked wild-caught mushrooms better than farm-grown ones. I'm going to have to decide what to do about foraging in general—maybe ban it."

"No!" I said.

She looked a little stunned at my first policy request. "What?" she asked, slightly irritated.

"The whole reason I became the Fungus Lord was because our family had trouble feeding ourselves." That was most of the truth, anyway. "I figured if I could recognize mushrooms, we could supplement our diet. I don't know if you've ever been hungry—"

"Believe me," Lynn said. "I have."

We looked at each other.

"The whole problem of governance comes when making dividing lines between a bunch of fuzzy groups that aren't cleanly divided to begin with. So let's say I allow families to forage for themselves. Sure. No problem in principle. Does it apply to hunting, too? What if wild game is depleted because people won't stop hunting? What if a family *does* kill large game, but can't eat it all? Do I just let the food go to waste? Can they sell the meat to make ends meet? If they can, why can't a whole business of hunters do the same?"

"I don't know," I admitted. "But letting people starve is wrong."

"I know. Believe me, I know."

"You've... been hungry, too?"

For once, she looked away. "One of my first goals was to stamp out world hunger. I.E. 7: All Imperial citizens have a right to food and water. I'm almost finished eradicating it. But I know, no matter how good the system, there's always cracks that people slip through."

"So..."

"So it's always more complicated than it seems at first glance. Yes, Mike, I realize if I make a decision banning certain kinds of foraging, it could hurt people like your family. It's also very likely that if I make a different decision, someone else would be badly hurt, or even killed. And if I make no decision at all, people would still be hurt. But I'll keep your words in mind."

"All right."

Then she sat up ramrod straight. "Sorry. Crisis starting. We'll talk again later." She hurried out.

"Bye," I called, but I heard no reply.

I sat back, but knew that wherever she had just gone, she had taken my heart with her.

"I'm losing it," I said out loud.

3

THE MARATHON

"Hey, Mike," Lynn said after an episode. "What do you think about a marathon?"

"Like binge watch a whole season at once?" I asked.

"Why not?"

"Aren't you super busy?"

"It would actually be easier for me to take a whole day off then parcel out time over a while," Lynn said, then smiled. "Remembrance Day is three days from now, anyway."

This was definitely a step forward in our whatever-we-were. "Sure," I said, a little disconcerted. "What do you want to watch?"

"I don't know. You pick."

"More Gundam? *Gundam Wing* is really good."

Lynn got out her cellphone and looked it up. "I don't know. 52 episodes is a lot."

"I'm sure you've already seen it, but how about *Death Note*? It's just two seasons, I think."

"Actually, I haven't," Lynn mused. "Does it live up to the hype?"

"Yep, it's worth a rewatch for me."

She looked up. "Looks like it's actually three cours. 37 episodes—we'll have to start early."

"No problem. How early is early?"

Lynn tilted her head in thought. "If we're serious about this, 4 AM."

I thought about it. We would spend the whole day, but wouldn't it be worth it to put a smile on Lynn's face? Or, for that matter, to spend that much time with her? "Sure. Where do we meet?"

"I'll show up at your apartment. They won't be able to find us, and I'll make sure no one can bother us."

"Deal."

My alarm blared, forcing me to wake. I looked at the time. 4 AM? Oh, wait. Yeah. That was today.

I got dressed and went to the door just as Lynn knocked on it. I opened to see her with a mischievous smile. In the air around her floated a stack of DVDs, a big bottle of soda, and a stack of pizza boxes.

"I didn't know there were pizza places open this early," I admitted.

"There aren't. I just phased over to some place that was and commandeered some random orders. Not even sure what's on these. Anyway, nice place you got here."

"Uh, yeah." This is *your* place, really, I didn't say. "We should get started."

"Yes, let's!"

We headed to the living room where Lynn pulled up a chair, and I took the couch.

Death Note is the story of Light Yagami, a high school student who finds a notebook that can magically kill anyone whose name is written in it. Our erstwhile protagonist then uses this to try to "fix" the world by murdering bad people. Light then slowly descends into madness as he becomes more and more extreme to accomplish his goals.

Lynn was hooked on the first episode. Her usual commentary drifted off. She became quieter and quieter, until eventually she was only whispering names. I saw her nibble at pizza absently, and then not at all.

During a credits sequence she was staring at the screen with an unsteady expression.

Oh no. *Now* it hit me that maybe this was a bit too close to home. She, too, had tried to fix the world, even if she hadn't tried to make herself a god.

"You still good?"

"Yeah. I'm still good," she murmured.

Aside from bathroom breaks, we watched episodes back to back. For the first time since I met her, she had fallen silent. I stopped commenting, too, seeing how deeply Lynn was lost in the story. Or just...lost.

Hours passed, then more hours. The sun rose. I microwaved slices of pizza between episodes and brought her plates. She took them without a word. The only time she turned her eyes away from the TV was when I had to change DVDs.

Seventeen hours later, I was tired of sitting, but Lynn sat still with perfect focus.. Out of concern I took more and more glances at her, but she wasn't noticing me any more. I didn't dare interrupt her thoughts.

Our protagonist-turned-villain makes a fatal mistake in the last episode and is cornered by police. Mortally wounded, he flees, only for his quasi-demonic companion to write his name in a Death Note. The credits rolled as Light lay on the staircase, motionless and dead.

The screen returned to the menu.

Lynn snapped her fingers and an invisible hand brought her the remote. She pressed the off switch. "That. That was good." Then she started to cry.

Now what? "You all right?"

"No," she groaned. "No, I'm not."

Our eyes met and I saw something way beyond the melancholy catharsis of the show's ending.

"I..." She took a breath. "I'd heard of the book before. The notebook. Some magisters experimented with binding daemons to notebooks, that would use daemonic knowledge to find and kill whoever was written in. It's a total inconvenience. You might as well just give the order explicitly." She shuddered, and started crying more. "This—this isn't what it's like at all. But it *is.*"

I held my words. I wondered if I should hold *her*, but I could sort of tell she didn't want to be touched.

"Oh God. No one gets it. What it means to change the world, even at the cost of... everything. Even... even your own sanity..."

Holy Spirit, give me the words you want me to say to her, I prayed silently.

"I fudged the statistics," Lynn said. "A lot more people died in the War than my government says. They weren't all mine. But no one believes me..."

"They weren't all yours," I repeated.

She shook her head and wiped her face. "I... it's not like it's on the show. Not all clean and easy." Then she burst out crying again. "I... I had to have money."

"You had to have money?"

"I did. I had ex—ex—expenses. And I needed a lot of money. So I went to a casino and cheated." She drew a deep breath, as if this could steady her. "They caught me." She fell dead silent.

I thought of what to say. I had heard of the Five-of-a-Kind massacre on the news, even if it never officially happened. Evidence she was the Antichrist, some said, when they still could.

But now the Antichrist was in front of me with tear streaks on her face.

I finally just said, "You said they weren't all yours."

"Japanese is a weird command language," was the last normal thing she said. Then she almost started babbling. "You can be really specific or base it all on context—nothing wrong with that—a common choice—I just learned it because—it was easy, and look, look, once you pick you can't change—and I had made the endings right because Japanese always ends with a verb and there's tenses and I always use *nasai* because you have to let them know it's a command and and and and." She took a deep breath. "And there was a guy there I was fighting them off and he was a magister and I told my daemons to kill..." She stopped, then almost whispered. "I just told them to kill. And they... they misinterpreted it. Deliberately."

"I'm sorry."

"Over four hundred people. I just said the wrong word and they killed almost everyone in the building." She looked at me, her eyes showing a vast, infected boil of grief that had been lanced and all the pus was leaking out. "No one would ever believe me. They just assumed I killed everyone deliberately. So I made everyone forget."

"I believe you, Lynn."

"I... I had to fix the world," she said. "I couldn't stop at anything. I was the only one who *could*. Even if it meant killing people. Even if it meant becoming the world's most hated villain. I just had to save everyone. But... I can't bring back the dead." She started sobbing again.

If I said one critical word, she would break. And God alone knew what would happen if I said the wrong word. God alone also knew if I could ever look myself in a mirror again if I hurt someone this emotionally vulnerable, no matter what I thought of her. But what could I say?

Maybe it was better to say nothing.

Lynn snapped her fingers and a box of tissues appeared. She wiped her eyes. "Don't tell anyone."

"I won't. But surely they'd believe you if you said—"

"No! Because it's *my fault*!" she screamed.

We just sat there and looked at each other.

"It... it really was, wasn't it?" she asked, looking at me like a criminal pleading guilty to a judge.

"Lynn," I said. "I'm not Jesus Christ. I don't have the right to judge another human being. I don't think there's anything I can say that will bring you comfort, other than I'm... I'm not going to judge you."

Sheer relief flooded Lynn's face, if no less pain. She took a deep breath. "Thanks."

"You're welcome."

"I think I need to be alone."

"Feel free," I said. "I'll clean up."

"See you. *Ikimashou.*" She disappeared with a snap of her fingers.

I felt back on the couch. What I had just witnessed? What had we just done? Was she going to kill me tomorrow, because she couldn't let her weaknesses get out?

No. No, she had looked at me like a life preserver. How many things had she done that she couldn't tell *anyone* about? Witch-Queen or not, at the end of the day, she was still a human being. You can't kill another person without some consequence to your soul.

I looked at the clock: 9:57 PM, Imperial Time. St. Malachi had a midnight Mass for Remembrance Day. I would go there and pray for Lynn's salvation.

4

The Price

She canceled anime the next day, and the day after that. I didn't how she was feeling, but at least she still texted me. I didn't know what I was feeling, other than glad she wasn't technically ghosting me. Whatever we had shared had scared both of us.

"Are you all right?" Alexander Jameson asked me, raising a thin white eyebrow over his thick bifocals. I didn't know my grandparents too well, but I felt Alexander was one of them. His kind, soft words could always bring me peace.

We had borrowed a classroom in the educational wing of the Palace complex. For some highly important officials, it was apparently easier to put their kids in the Palace's own school than risk going outside.

Was *I* a highly-important official?

"I, uh, am struggling. I—" I caught myself. "How do you know if you're in love with someone?" The old theologian had started me off on God's love for us, fittingly thinking that if I didn't have that bashed into my head, no other theological fact would be meaningful.

"What kind of love?" he asked.

"*Eros*, romantic love." Now that I said it out loud, the truth both made more and less sense.

"It's not unreasonable for a man your age. Can I ask what her name is?"

I wondered if I should say it. To hell with it. "Lynn."

"Ah. That makes things more complicated. But then love is that way. If you're wondering if you're wrong to love her, no, love is never wrong. But it's worth considering whether it's the appropriate kind of love. Have you talked about it?"

"Sort of? She's been flirting back." Or was that my imagination?

"I see," he said gravely. "If you were just talking about a girl you'd met, I'd advise you to go ask her out. But it sounds like it's more than that, already."

"Yep. We've been 'dating,' for…" How long had it been? I had literally lost track of time. We started to binge watch, then that marathon…

"I think it's worth establishing at this point what she feels your relationship is. Or what she'd like it to be. It's better to have the uncomfortable conversation than to just try to imagine if you're starting to have serious thoughts."

I nodded. I had enough experience to know there's a difference between wanting something with a girl and both of you wanting something. "Yes, sir. Love is hard."

"It can be. Or it can be the most exciting adventure of your life. But whatever happens, I'd like you to think of this: however hard it is, however much you want her, no matter if she wants you back, that is still not how badly Jesus Christ wants *you.*"

I took a deep breath. Everything made so much more sense when I talked with him.

Then my phone went off. Caller ID: all nines. "Hold up, she's calling right now!" I hurried out into the hallway to answer. "Hello?"

"Hi, Mike. I've got good news and bad news. Bad news: I won't have free time for a few weeks. Huge crisis. But I can chat with you over lunch."

Chat with.

Not watch anime with.

Chat with.

"Great!" I said, my enthusiasm very real. "Where should I meet you?"

"One of the Palace eateries. None of them serve mushrooms, thankfully."

"I can still test your food."

"Perfect! I'll text you tomorrow with which one." A pause. "Oh no. Got to go *right now*—sorry!" She hung up.

I leaned against the wall.

Nope. Wasn't making it up. She *had* to be interested in me.

Right?

I had fitful nightmares that night of trying to talk to Lynn while people kept randomly interrupting with phone calls. My phone kept going off. Then I realized it was my phone, for serious.

I forced myself awake and grabbed the vibrating device. "Mike. What's up?"

"Are you alone?" Kyle asked softly.

"I'm in *bed*, Kyle. It's..." I looked at the alarm clock. "5 AM over here."

"I've been trying to reach you all day, I mean, since I got out."

"Got out?"

"They took everyone!"

"What?"

"I'm not joking! The SMP and a bunch of magisters showed up and told everyone to get in their trucks and leave right away."

"*What?* Kyle, if this is a joke..."

"Why the hell would I be wandering the wilderness of Tennessee at 11 PM in my PJs if I wasn't serious? I'm the only one who escaped." His voice was dead serious. "Ask your girlfriend about it. Tell her you won't be with her if she keeps hostages."

"What—"

"Got to keep moving. They're tracking me." He hung up.

I dialed Grandpa Franklin. Ring, ring, ring, no reply.

I texted Mom.

Mom, you OK?

No reply.

Now I was worried.

I looked at the clock. I wouldn't be able to go to daily Mass and see Lynn today, not while going through Palace security. God help me if I didn't talk to Lynn, today.

God help me *to* talk to Lynn.

If she had kidnapped my village to keep me locked in here—as ridiculous as that sounded when not talking to Kyle—she didn't show it. She stepped into the wide cafeteria and everyone bowed. Including me. "Hi, Mike. You're here early."

"Can I talk to you in private?" I asked, heart hammering.

"Sure?" She motioned for me to follow.

The Palace was full of doors, most of them unmarked. She opened one to show me an empty room with a giant daemonic inscription on the floor. "What's up?" she asked.

"What did you do to my village?"

"That's an awfully specific accusation," she said, eyes looking into mine. "Why would you make it?"

"It's an awfully specific question, which you aren't answering."

"True. By why would you think to ask it?"

"Enough games—"

"I was hoping we could have this conversation later," she said with a sigh. "The best-laid plans, and all that."

I tried to breathe calmly. "What happened?"

"We had to evacuate them."

"Why isn't anyone answering the phone?"

"We had to be sure."

"Of what?"

She stared into my eyes with her usual intensity.

"I want an answer, Lynn."

"I can give you one," she said, unmoving and unmoved. "But you aren't going to be talking about it to anyone—not the press, not your family, not anyone else."

"Understood."

"Follow me." She got up and took off at a brisk speed to the elevator. I stepped inside with her and found myself within hand-holding distance.

What would happen if I touched her?

Or if she touched me?

She pressed a high number, and within a few seconds we arrived.

I followed her deeper and deeper into the Palace, passing increasingly vociferous warnings about unauthorized entry. At some point the signage replaced legal consequences with lethal ones. I hurried to keep up.

We stopped by a sign that said "Special Magical Police, Main Department." She snapped her fingers and the door opened on its own.

I followed her inside and it slammed behind us.

I didn't know to expect a bunch of cubicles, but that's what I saw: a giant office. Doors were carefully shut, though, and as we passed I tried not to see anything that would get me in more trouble.

More?

We came to another door, labeled "CHIEF POUL ARMSTRONG" and Lynn waltzed right in. "Ah, Darius, I didn't expect to see you here."

Darius Janus was sitting across from an older, overweight man, who had the overwhelming aura of a man who doesn't *need* to look threatening. I had met him before, at the reception after the ceremony, but by his inquisitive look I felt like we had just met. "Lynn, we have had discussions about bringing your Companions in here," Poul Armstrong said.

If the Imperatrix Mundi was offended at being scolded, she didn't show it. "He has Level 3 clearance as a Companion and you two can interview him afterwards. Besides, he already knows—something, at least."

"I did want to talk to you about your experience with the water," Darius said, regarding me with a curious expression. "I assume you're here to see the tape?"

"The tape?" I asked, feeling more out of my depth by the minute. I didn't even know Level 3 clearance was a thing, let alone that I had it. It must have been on a paper I didn't read too closely.

Poul Armstrong, with the slow, careful movement of the arthritic, opened a drawer and pulled out a disk, which he inserted into a projector. "Lynn, if you would turn off the lights?"

Lynn snapped her fingers and the lights dimmed.

One wall, clear of trophies or books, showed the cameraman following a pair of magisters, what I assumed was a plainclothes policewoman, and—very unnervingly—Marty Mac, the old fisherman, walking up to a pier by the pond near Lumberton. "The crazy thing is," my old friend said. "The fish always seem to be fine. Can't get anyone to eat them, but I tried a bite myself and they didn't taste any different."

"Do you have any specimens?" a magister asked.

"Not right now, but I can get you one real quick. Ha! Reel."

"Do we have time?" the other magister asked.

"The Witch-Queen wants this investigated," the SMP agent replied. "I guess we're going fishing today."

And so as Marty got out his rod and fished, talking incessantly to the three, my sense of reality warped more and more. That was Marty, right? This wasn't some elaborate staged scene—

"Ah, here we go!" He reeled up a small goldfish. "Nasty buggers. Some poor kid thought was easier to release them than to kill them, and now they're eatin' up the ecosystem—go tell that to the Witch-Queen, would ya?"

"I'll be sure to let her know," the magister said impatiently.

"Here, see for yourself." Marty offered him the goldfish. "Perfectly harmless."

Logging is an industry with occasionally gruesome accidents. I'd seen a man crushed under a log once, although we got him to medical attention fast enough he was only crippled. I had also seen a man lose a leg due to a chainsaw. It still wasn't preparation for that bloody instant when the magister took the goldfish and it exploded.

"James!" the other magister screamed. James was also screaming. The cameraman staggered back. The hazy outlines of powerful daemons appeared, but no further attack came. A first aid kit popped into existence and those who still had two hands helped the other two.

I couldn't watch or look away.

"Jesus!" James swore, gritting his teeth. "Harmless as—" His oath was interrupted by another louder oath as the SMP agent wrapped a bandage.

Marty looked remarkably calm, for having lost a hand. "Hell, guess they weren't so safe after all. Ow! God, ow! That hurts!"

"HQ, we need immediate medivac at coordinates..." the SMP agent rattled off numbers.

"What else has been drinking the water?" someone asked.

"Good Lord, if this was in people..." the cameraman said.

"We've seen enough," the SMP agent shouted. "Get away from the water!"

They hurried the magister and Marty off the pier.

Armstrong stopped the video. "I wouldn't suppose you would be interested in the rest, unless you sincerely want to see field surgery."

"I'll pass. Are they OK? I know the fisherman."

"They're both still alive, if that's what you're wondering," Lynn said. "I ordered state-of-the-art prosthetics for both of them. But you do realize what you saw, right?"

"A bomb that only goes off on magisters?"

"Correct," Darius acknowledged. "We haven't experimented, obviously, but we believe that the daemons inside the tainted water are bound to be triggered by the usual criteria for anti-personnel daemons."

I breathed deeply. "So you had to evacuate everyone."

"Very, very, carefully, and without making a fuss," Lynn said. "Everyone in your village who wasn't boiling water is a proximity mine to magisters. I'm amazed no one died already."

"Thank God," I said, feeling relief. So it wasn't about me.

Wait though— "Get back!" I shouted.

They all looked at me. "I drank that stuff, too!"

"Mike," Lynn said with a raised eyebrow. "Don't you think if you still had it in your system, you would have exploded already?

"Oh. Yeah."

"The body eliminates the protein relatively quickly," Darius explained. "The citizens of the various nearby villages are currently in a holding facility while it passes naturally."

"Villages? Plural?"

"Lynn," Armstrong said softly. "This is what happens every time you bring a Companion in. Someone here says something and a leak begins."

A Companion? What? Before I could ask Lynn had already spoke, unmoved. "Yeah, well, you need to be a bit more careful with leaks on your end, because he already knew."

The two powerful men looked at me.

"Yeah, uh, a friend told me they had taken everyone. And that he ran away."

Armstrong raised an eyebrow, and began writing notes. "When did you get the call?"

"This morning."

"What is his name?" Darius asked.

"Kyle Franklin. He's, um, weird. Please don't punish him."

"I would be more concerned for your friend in that the moment he reaches civilization there is a remote chance that he will demolish a building. We don't know what else triggers the demodaemons."

"*Kyle Franklin ikiteiru ka?*" Lynn asked out loud. "He's still alive. I take he's not a magister?"

"He wants to be one, but, uh, he has strong opinions about the Empire."

"Don't we all?" Darius asked dryly.

Lynn didn't react. "The problem is that if we send a magister to find him, he'll go boom. Does he have survival skills?"

"He thinks he does. And I don't *think* he drank any of the tainted water. He definitely likes to fish, though."

The three around me fell silent.

"Lynn, I suggest you and Darius discuss the daemonological aspects. I need to talk with your Companion some more," Armstrong said.

"All right," Lynn agreed. "Don't worry, Mike, he doesn't bite. Darius, with me."

They left, leaving me alone in the room with the Chief.

"So, uh, I guess it was a good thing that Lynn brought me in?" I ventured.

"Do you personally believe your friend is involved with any kind of daemonology, authorized or not?" Armstrong asked.

"No, sir. Well..." Oh dear God, how had I ended up about to narc on my best friend to the chief of the SMP? "I think he once got out some diagrams and tried to figure it out himself."

"Did he have access to gravitational gear?"

"Not that I know of. We're really poor out in Lumberton."

"Does he have access to a carpenter's equipment?"

"What?"

"Levels, plumb lines, measurement tools?"

"Why?" I asked. "I mean, his dad's a carpenter, but..."

"An informed rogue magister can make do with nothing more than a laser pointer, a straight edge, a pencil and a plumb line."

I fell silent.

"Let me explain the situation. While you, as an Imperial citizen, have a right not to self-incriminate, that does not apply to incriminating your friends and acquaintances. You could be called to court to testify against him. But we have some discretion due to our nature as, to put it bluntly, the secret police. If he is nothing more than a poseur then we can overlook this. But if he actually summoned a daemon, then he is in serious trouble."

I remained silent.

"Is he a poseur?"

"If he really summoned something then he would never shut up about it." Or would he? He would tell me about it, at least. "I don't think, even if he tried, he ever succeeded."

"I am told that binding a daemon is a unique experience, and like all relation-ships has a price. So I would very much expect, based on what you have told me, that he is innocent of crimes under our jurisdiction."

I breathed easier.

How much was Kyle worth to me?

How much was Lynn?

Then it hit me. "I think I can call him back."

"That would be greatly helpful. While you're here, I might as well hear straight from you about your experiences with the water."

"It's not much to talk about, I'm sure," I told him. "It just tasted brackish, and, well, we didn't think it was anything at first…"

After Armstrong I talked to Darius, repeating the same information. It seemed he had heard more or less the same facts. "It's kinda crazy," I admitted. "If the village hadn't sent me…" We would have never gotten help, until one of us blew up a building. And I would never have met Lynn.

"I can tell you why your local magisterium was ignoring you," Darius said. "Daemons do not grow in power. The fact that the problem was growing worse implies it was not a daemon."

"But it *was* a daemon."

"To be accurate, it was many daemons. The Rank IV we discovered was pro-ducing a certain kind of complex protein by decomposing nutrients in the water and soil, with which it bound an endless number of Rank Is. We suspect the perpetrator did not realize the protein in large numbers would taste brackish, because by doing so his scheme was exposed."

"You think it's one person?"

"I am telling you the daemonological aspects of the matter, in order that you may be able to provide better information," he said firmly. "The rest of the investigation is not your concern."

"Sorry, sir."

"But on that note, a bound daemon always has one master. There is one powerful magister who bound a Rank V or a Rank VI who caused this whole mess. You see, we found other, identical daemons elsewhere in the subdominion, which implies the existence of a mother daemon to the Rank IV mother daemons. This is the most sophisticated work of biodaemonology I have ever seen. And whoever bound the original daemon has no care for how many corpses pile up. An attitude that *many* high magisters share." He glanced elsewhere.

"Are you accusing Lynn of—"

"That's a remarkably dangerous question to ask in the headquarters of the Special Magical Police."

Well, *duh*. "Uh..." I found I was fidgeting.

"The Imperatrix knows I have objections to our present circumstances. And she knows I consider her personally responsible for all the deaths of the War. But consider this very incident: if we do nothing, people will die. And a very large number at that."

"Oh." My hands hurt from squeezing.

"You see, these daemons are part of what we call an Summoning Minus Termination scenario: a legion of daemons that keeps growing endlessly. Since the early days of daemonology, the practice has been banned. It's simply far too dangerous. This is not an act of defiance, this is indiscriminate terrorism."

"I see."

"I am sorry we had to evacuate your village. But we cannot take chances."

"I... understand."

"Now if you'll excuse me, I have some daemonology scheduled today and must get to it promptly. If you have any other questions, or a thought comes to you, please let me know."

"I will," I promised.

I stepped out to see me a young man waiting for me. "Ryan Wings," he intro-duced himself. "Are you Michael Mason?"

"I am."

"Do you go by Mike or Michael?"

"Mike, usually. Who are you?"

"I'm a negotiator with the SMP," he said. "My job is to get everyone out of this situation alive."

What the hell had I gotten myself into? Or had Kyle gotten himself into? "What's happening?"

"Right now, he's somewhere in the wilderness of Tennessee. We could track him down with magisters, but that will likely set him off. At this moment, he might be sleeping, or he might still be wandering. So what I want to do is talk with you, learn about him, and then we'll call him together."

"Sounds like a plan."

"If he learns that he can potentially explode, what will he do?"

I thought about it. "He never struck me as suicidal, but he might be tempted to do something dumb."

"Known him for a while?"

"He's my best friend..." We would talk as we fished in the pond, about God, his latest conspiracy theories, anime, gaming... We had both gotten busy with our lives, and then the Witch-Queen came. He was never OK after that.

Hours later, we sat around a conference room with two more SMP agents. A magister helped me move my SIM card to a special phone covered with daemonic inscriptions.

"Our daemons can track his exact location when you call," Ryan explained. "If we can get him to peacefully surrender, that's great. If he throws his phone away, we have no way of tracking him, but he can't run far."

"What do you want me to say?" I asked.

"Be yourself."

"All right," I said. "When do we begin?"

"Whenever you're ready."

Please, God, I prayed. I dialed Kyle.

He answered immediately. "Where are you?"

"Somewhere in the Palace—"

"No! Get out of there! They'll hunt you down and pump you for information. I know they're after the mother daemon, right? And they think you know where she is. But—"

"Kyle!" I interrupted. "You are a living proximity mine."

"What?"

"That water contains demodaemons or something. If you touch a magister you go boom."

"...That's what they *want* you to think."

"Excuse me, Kyle, can I call you Kyle?" Ryan interrupted.

"Who are you?" Kyle asked, instantly suspicious.

"My name's Ryan. What's going on?"

"The Witch-Queen has her stiletto on the world's throat!"

Actually, she wore flats, but before I could note that, Ryan already answered. "Yeah, I know. I was on the other side, once."

"What?" Kyle asked, suddenly unsure.

"I worked with MagiPol until after the War."

"You're with the SMP now?" Kyle asked.

"I am."

"Traitor!" he shrieked so loudly the phone's mic cut out.

I opened my mouth, but Ryan shook his head. Over the next half-hour, we listened to Kyle rant incoherently about America, the Witch-Queen, and any number of contradictory conspiracy theories. Every now and then Ryan would trigger him again, deliberately, until Kyle's breath was ragged and he was sobbing.

"Hey, listen, man," Ryan said. "Mike's right. You've got demodaemons in your blood. Step next to a magister and you'll go boom. We don't know what else might set you off."

Silence.

"I can't do anything about the Witch-Queen, but I can make sure neither you nor any innocents die."

"There... there are no innocents," Kyle said softly.

"Did you know what happened to Marty Mac?" I asked on instinct.

"What?"

"I saw it on tape. A goldfish blew off his hand."

A deeper silence.

"I'm a Jew," Ryan said. "I know that no one is really perfect in God's eyes. You're right, no one is really innocent. But what I do know is we can live in a world where more people live the rest of their lives."

Kyle hung up.

"Great." I facepalmed.

Ryan shrugged. "It happens."

A magister had been making notes on a map of Tennessee. "He's pretty far from civilization."

"Yeah, but he's close to the edge of the interdict zone," the other agent said. "If he spreads the daemons—"

"Not possible," the magister said. "He doesn't have a mother daemon."

"Still could go off on someone."

Ryan, meanwhile, jotted down a number on a piece of paper. "Text Kyle this number and keep your phone with you. He might call me, he might call you, he might call no one. We'll try again in a bit."

"My mind is shot," I said.

"How about some pizza?" he offered.

"Sure thing."

Ryan, it turned out, was not merely Jewish, but a convert to Judaism. Pretty soon we were talking about our own life stories. His entire job revolved around talking to people and calming them down, but honestly he could have been a therapist, too.

I had texted Kyle—and he had read the message—but no reply.

The room stilled, and then everyone stood. Lynn had just entered. She went up to us, took a slice of pizza from the box we were eating, and started scarfing it down. She snapped her fingers and a soda appeared in her hands, which she downed. "Mike, a word?" she asked.

I followed her out to another office. I noticed the same inscription as the previous quiet room, this time on the ceiling.

"We have your friend in custody," she told me. "Right now I'm having him moved to the same facility as the rest of your village."

"That was quick."

"We couldn't risk him going off," she explained. "He had so many demodaemons in him he was visible on a gravity mapper. When the agents met up with him, he threatened to summon daemons, which, by the way, proved he was not a magister."

"How so?"

"You summon a daemon you don't have bound, you manifest a daemon you *do* have bound. Terminology aside, he's just a young man with anger issues and a mouth."

"That describes Kyle." I sighed. "Will you let him go?"

"I don't know yet. If he cooperates, I'll pardon him. If not, he can make the stand he wants so badly."

I didn't know what to say. At last, to break the silence, I asked, "When will you let my village go?"

"When we're sure all the proteins in their bodies have degraded. It will be a case-by-case basis, depending on how much of the tainted water they drank and what kind of poisoned animal flesh or plants they digested. In young Mr. Magister-Wannabe-With-a-Mouth's case, it may be some time. He has enough of the protein in him to flatten a city block."

Dear God, I had no idea. Lynn said all those things calmly and matter-of-fact-ly, without breaking eye contact. To her, a threat this terrible was too common to be upset about. Or else she had a will made of a titanium-steel alloy.

"When will we get back to Lumberton?"

"When we find the mother daemon. I don't know when that will be. It may be months. It may be years. The SMP has unsolved cases of magical terrorism dating back to the beginning of my reign. But I promise you, I will not stop looking until we find it."

"It affected other villages, too, they said."

"Yes. We're evacing the whole region. Towns ten times the size of yours, abandoned." And again, she didn't break eye contact. "It's a terrible choice, I admit. But the other options are all far worse."

"I..." I paused, feeling as if one more word would deorbit me into the black hole that was Lynn. "I understand." I could practically feel the gravitational pull.

"Good. By the way, we've cut off communications for the moment, but I can get notes passed back and forth between you and your mom."

"Thanks." But so many others would only know that their loved ones had disappeared without a trace.

5

The Flames of Hope

M om's handwriting was a little shaky, and there wasn't a lot of room on the paper.

> We're OK over here, but a little disturbed. They told us not to talk about what's going on. Nothing awful.

> We haven't seen Marty Mac or Kyle Franklin. They said they're in a different part of the facility. We all have our rooms, but we can't leave and they don't want us congregating.

> Keep praying for us — Mom

I took a deep breath, but I wasn't relieved. What exactly were the SMP doing to get the proteins out? Did they assume they would leave the body naturally, like they apparently had in me? Or were they taking additional measures? I didn't want to think what additional measures would look like.

So I didn't. I headed to the Palace gym and worked out.

As a lumberjack I usually didn't need to deliberately exercise as much, but to stay fit I went regularly. The place had the unduly sharp smell of daemonical-ly-cleaned vinyl, and the music was the most obnoxious of heavy rock, but the familiar workout equipment was one of the few things I *did* know in my new world.

I'd heard magisters could make themselves thin, but I didn't think they could make themselves buff, at least after I recognized some magisters I'd seen around the Palace. Several personal trainers moved around to help out, but I hadn't availed myself of anyone except a spotter.

I kept my cellphone near me just in case Lynn called.

When it went off, I set down the weights and they immediately flew off to the racks. I sighed, felt through my bag, and flipped my phone open.

Then I frowned. I didn't recognize the caller ID: someone somewhere in the Mid-North German Dominion.

A scam call? But why would a scammer call from so far away?

Curious, I answered.

"Is this Michael Mason?" a young man with a German accent asked.

"Yes. Who is this?"

"This is Fritz Kempf. I saw your article in *Nobility Today*."

"What?"

"I'm just calling to tell you that the money doesn't last. You have to save for when she... tires of you."

"Who the hell are you?"

"I was one of her Companions."

Dread flooded me. "Companions," I repeated.

"She said she loved plants, like I did. We had all sorts of plants together. Even rare and near-extinct ones. But then she got bored of it and dismissed me. I did not have enough room or money left to store them all. Some were..." And he began weeping.

"Excuse me, by 'she' do you mean...?"

"Lynn. Yes."

I had nothing to say.

"There's a number of us. We've formed a kind of society. She had fun with each of us for a month or two, then got bored. The money doesn't last—"

"I don't care about the *money!*" I snapped.

"But you should! You don't get it. It doesn't last—"

"I. Don't. Care!" I screamed and threw my cellphone at the wall. The case cracked.

I sighed, walked over to it as others watched awkwardly, and saw the tiny screen had cracked again, too. It was still on. "Sir," I heard. I hung up.

Immediately he called again.

I hung up again and turned my phone off.

Damn it.

I sat down and held my head, more emotions flooding through me than water through the Amazon.

I didn't care about the money.

Right.

But wasn't that the whole reason I was here and not with my village in some containment facility? The whole reason I consented to being her pretend boyfriend.

Pretend boyfriend.

Now I had proof.

Or did I? Hope seemed too painful to handle, like a piece of cookware that had been heated with a blowtorch. I badly wanted to believe Lynn truly was interested in me, but... I felt like my heart was being torn in two.

Whatever. If she was trying to buy my heart, she wouldn't succeed. What would I donate to today? A religious order? Perhaps a charity? Yes, a charity. My stormy soul calmed a little. I'd shower, head home, head to the Imperial Bank, and I'd... not think about it in the meantime.

If I could.

I opened my mailbox and picked a spam letter at random. The Red Cross. Why not?

I stepped outside of my apartment complex and hopped on a trolley. I felt slow relief as we reached the Imperial Bank branch. I stepped inside and before I had even reached the line a teller flagged me down. "Mr. Mason, I can help you."

Being Companion had its perks... for now.

"Hello," I said. "I'd like to send money to the Red Cross. I don't know how much money I have—" Oh my God how could I just *say* that?

"Of course, sir." She whispered something, and the typewriter by her clacked. She frowned.

"Excuse me?"

"I'm very sorry, sir, I must consult with my manager. If you would wait?"

"Of... of course." I said. She whispered and stood there with a placid smile.

What was going on? Did Lynn just get tired of me, and this was the end? My chest tightened as if holding my heart back from exploding. That botanist "ex" could have just been making it up, right? What if... I didn't know. I couldn't think of a hypothetical.

Another woman arrived. "Are you Michael Mason?"

"I am."

"I'm very sorry, but a hold has been placed on your account. We can't transfer any money in or out, except for up to 100 IM in cash."

"Why?"

"Compliance flagged your account for suspicious activity."

"I've barely used it!"

"I don't know, sir. It happens all the time, for anything from too many transfers out—"

"Jesus Christ, all of those were voluntary!" I snapped, then immediately regretted it. But my anger burst forth all the more. "What the hell, do you think I was money laundering?"

"I'm very sorry, sir, but we can't release the funds until Compliance says so."

I felt rage building within me, but I wrestled control back over myself. No. These people had nothing to do it. No shooting the messenger. "All... right." I took slow breaths. "I'd... I'd... I'd like to withdraw 100 IM."

"Of course, sir."

"Mike! Where were you? I called three times and no answer."

I turned to see Her Imperial Majesty herself, with a ticked-off expression.

"Oh, hi, Lynn, I, uh, was trying to transfer money. Could you help here?" I asked calmly, as if everything was all right.

"To whom?" She raised an eyebrow.

"Just a charity."

"Why didn't you answer your phone?"

"I, uh, had turned it off. Look, can you sort this out?"

"What's going on?" she asked the teller.

"I'm very sorry, Your Imperial Majesty. Compliance had put a hold on the account because of suspicious transfers. We can remove it immediately."

She looked the teller in the eyes. "What transfers?"

"One moment, ma'am."

"Wait, I, uh, can explain—" I said, but not before invisible hands had typed up a statement.

Lynn took it, then frowned. Then frowned some more. "*This* is what you've been spending money on?"

"It's my money," I protested.

She stared me down. "I gave it to you so you could spend on it on yourself. If I wanted it to go to some random charity I would have given directly or as an Imperial Grant."

"—Sorry." I said at last.

She sighed. "Get a better suit. The Needle's Eye has a special on Taiwanese cusine tomorrow, and I've been looking forward to it."

"Yes, ma'am."

"Good."

"Lynn, I have a quest—" I caught myself. The one thing I wasn't prepared for was the truth: what if this was all just a role-playing game for her, and I was simply part of the cast? "Never mind."

"What?"

"Forget it. I'll buy a better suit."

"Good." She tilted her head. "Oh crud crisis bye! *Ikimashou.*" She snapped her fingers and disappeared.

I wandered the streets of the Capital in a daze. I passed by a street stall selling something that smelled delicious. I took another street. I had already eaten.

And I didn't want to spend any more money.

How had my life gone so wrong so fast?

I passed by a store and just saw a glance of a magazine stand inside.

I thought about it, then went in.

Nobility Today had a photo of me at Mass on the front page, a photo I didn't remember being taken. I pulled it off the rack and went to the counter.

The bored young woman scanned the magazine. "One—Oh, you're the Companion!" she squealed. "OH EM GEE! This is amazing! Will you sign something for me?!"

"Uh, I don't think I'm allowed to."

"Ah. Shame. Have a nice day!" She smiled brightly.

I hurried outside to find a bench and read the article on me.

> Michael Mason's spending habits turn to the charitable, despite
> coming from a poor background. Unlike most Companions,
> we haven't seen him at the auction house. Sources say that he
> in fact has been giving immense amounts to random charities.
> Meanwhile, what about his family? Recently a chunk of the
> Tennessee Subdominion was placed under an Imperial inter-

dict. Duke Edgeworth declined to comment. Our sources tell
us that no one has heard—

I felt so sick I couldn't keep going. I walked—stumbled, more like—to the
nearest trashcan and insulted it and its contents by tossing the magazine inside.

"I didn't *want* the money," I said, stumbling away. "I just..."

I just wanted to have some fun with a cute girl who liked anime.

Now everything was ruined. I had become a noble in all but title.

I looked around and found I had taken my usual path out of habit. I was right
outside of St. Malachi's.

I stepped inside.

In the vestibule, I spotted a wall of donor plaques. I could have had one, I
realized. I donated such a huge sum of money...

I tore myself away and wandered into the nave. I looked at the poor box and
felt almost a palpable revulsion. I walked, directionless, deeper in.

Then I saw Fr. Xavier praying before the St. Joseph statue. Yes, I needed to
go to Confession. I'd just pray here for a bit until confessions started.

But I couldn't concentrate on prayer at all. When I got in line, I could do
little more than chant the name of Jesus. "Jesus. Jesus. Jesus." Of course, some
thought whispered in my mind, why would he listen to his name when you
misuse it?

No, that was the devil talking. I kept chanting the Holy Name.

The guy in front of me in the confession line left and I walked in.

"In the name of the Father and the Son and the Holy Spirit."

"Bless me, Father, for I have sinned. It's been a week, I think. Father, I... took
the name of Jesus in vain. I got really angry at people who didn't deserve my
anger, and... well, maybe I should start somewhere earlier."

"Certainly."

"There's... a girl."

"I see. What about her?"

"She may or may not be paying me to be her pretend boyfriend."

I heard only silence for two seconds. "What?"

"I mean, I don't know," I admitted.

"You don't know if she's paying you?"

"I know she's paying me!" My voice raised. "That's the problem. It's too much money."

"First of all, I would assume that if someone is paying you to be in a relationship, it would be artificial to begin with."

"See, I would think that, but... I think she's actually into me. Except one of her... exes... told me he..."

"Let's just slow down. Do you believe she loves you? Or is at least interested in you?"

"She's at least interested in me. I think. I... I don't care about the money."

"But there's too much of it?"

"I know. It's ridiculous," I snapped. "I get paid more every week then I used to make in a year. Then I tried giving it away, but then they put a hold on my account. And she didn't lift it!"

"How could your girlfriend-or-not lift it to begin with? Is she a noble?"

"Uh. Yes."

"I ask, not to pry, but because I meet a lot of couples with class issues. Nobles marrying commoners or nobles of higher rank. Or magisters marrying mundanes. I would ask if you are really being paid to be her boyfriend, or if you're simply interpreting events based on your relative social standings."

I thought about it, back to the day she had popped into my hotel room. She had talked about just paying me to be an anime watching buddy, so I could support my family. Then she had called it a gift.

Had she ever demanded anything of me? Or had she simply wanted to have fun with me?

"I... don't know," I thought out loud. "But it's too much money. I'm not greedy."

"All you've talked about so far is money."

I barely resisted the urge to blaspheme again. "I see," I said instead. "But I can't tithe it or anything!"

"Do you know what the Lord originally commanded the Holy People to do, regarding tithing?"

"Bring it to the priests and Levites?"

"Not quite. He told them to bring the first-fruits of their produce to the Tabernacle, or later, the Temple, and eat it there before him. And if that was logistically impossible, sell it for money, bring the money there, and then buy whatever their hearts desired, and eat it before the Lord, and rejoice."

"I... OK. I can do that. I think."

"Good. For your penance, read and pray over Deuteronomy chapter 14. I *suggest* you listen to the wisdom contained in it. Now will you make an Act of Contrition?"

"Is that all?" I asked.

"The fact that you're violently resisting spending money on yourself is a good sign that you badly need to. Your girlfriend, or whoever she is, would very much like it if you spent that money on what brought *you* happiness, right?"

"Right. I'm sorry."

"It's not a *sin*. But there are many forms of greed, just as there are many forms of envy and pride. Money is not evil. It's just a tool. Enjoy it."

"Yes, sir."

"Now will you make your Act of Contrition?"

"Oh my God, I am heartily sorry for offending you..." And Lynn, for that matter. Maybe God was subtly trying to tell me to relax about money, before it became a bigger problem.

Yes, I decided. I would just buy *something*.

But my resolve drained immediately on stepping out of St. Malachi's. Maybe I should just save money.

Or maybe that was the devil talking. After all, I had spent an entire conversation on nothing but money. Both anorexics and gluttons were obsessed with food.

Screw it. A tithe was 10%, right? So what could I spent 10% of 200,000 IM on?

A car? A pickup truck?

But how would I get it back to Lumberton, if Lumberton was even a place anymore?

No, not time to think about that. I wandered towards the shopping district.

Colorful advertisements sprang out from stores, advertising everything from snacks to jewelry. I could get Mom something really nice—no, that wasn't myself. And *I* certainly wasn't that interested in jewelry.

But what on Earth would cost that much?

Maybe I would buy several things? How about a gaming computer and a VR headset? Or—I stopped as I saw it.

I stood in front of a cellphone store, with smartphones in the window.

This was ridiculous. Daemon-proof smartphones were ridiculously expensive. But wasn't it ridiculous that I thought so much about money?

Besides, I really did need a new cellphone.

I forced myself inside.

Nearly everyone inside was a magister, including the saleswoman. "Welcome! How can I help you?"

"I'd... I'd like to buy a smartphone," I stammered.

"You've come to the right place." She smiled. "What kind were you looking for?"

"I don't know. I've never done this before."

"No need to worry. We can suggest..."

And before long I was candidly ignoring the price tags on everything she had to offer. I felt as if I was in kind of surreal dream where every number had a bunch of extra zeroes.

"We can, of course, bind a daemon to your phone for only another 4,000 IM."

"You need to bind a daemon to one?" I asked.

"It's what makes them 'daemon-proof,' although that name is pretty inaccurate," she explained. "In any case, our services involve no contractual or daemonological obligation on your part. We just bind the daemon and you walk home with a new phone."

"Sur—" Whoa, whoa, hold on. I bet the Imperial Government wouldn't be too happy about me bringing some random daemon into the Palace. "I'll need someone else to do it."

"Of course. But mind you, we can give you a discount if..."

"No, no, really, I... work in government."

"Ah, I see. No need to worry, then. That should be everything. Just know that you can't use it at all until you've had a daemon bound to it."

"Got it."

The final bill was 18,400 IM. I had studiously rejected any idea of a payment plan. "Do I write a check or...?"

"We accept all major credit cards."

You know, when would I ever have the chance to use a freakin' credit card again? I dug through my wallet for the card. I could see her eyes widen just slightly at it. She clapped her hands and a card reader appeared in her hands. "Just insert it."

I inserted it. BEEP! "*Please remove card,*" the screen read.

I pulled it back out.

"*Transaction approved.*"

"It was a pleasure doing business with you," the saleswoman said with a smile. "If you need anything, just call."

"I will," I promised.

Back at my apartment, I called Alice on my old phone. "I think I need a bit of daemonology."

"Have you ever met a magister?"

"Uh... sort of?"

"That sort of question will get you dirty looks. Even 'a bit' of daemonology is expensive. But I assume you have a specific need?"

"I bought a smartphone, and I figured I probably couldn't just have someone random person it set up."

"You would be correct. In that case, I'd talk to Lynn. She'd want to do it herself."

"Thanks," I said. "Wait, can you come by for a minute?"

"One moment." I heard Latin. "I'm outside your door."

I opened it to find her. "It's..." Did I dare ask? No, I had already come this far.

"It's...?" she repeated.

"Who am I, really?"

"Let's talk inside."

My heart sank as we walked to the living room. "One of Lynn's... 'exes' talked to me."

"I wondered when you would find out," she said with a sigh. "It always happens eventually."

My heart sank deeper than the *Bismarck*.

"It's true, to an extent. Lynn occasionally has moods of severe loneliess. She'll pick someone seemingly at random to be a Companion for a month or two. We've had the astrophysicist, the painter, the exotic botanist—we had all sorts of plants around the Palace when he was here."

"He told me about being unable to store them all."

"Yes, I felt bad about it, too. But Lynn had gotten fed up with him."

"So..."

"But you're the longest-lasting Companion she's ever had. And she's constantly talking about you to me."

My heart rose higher than the Saturn V.

"Are you different?" She shrugged. "Lynn's a mystery, even to me. But let me tell you one thing: as long as Lynn's content, the world is safer. She hasn't—well, I can't talk about it. But she's had less violent moods lately."

"I didn't know she had violent moods."

"She very much does, when she gets angry."

I smacked my palm to my forehead.

"What?"

"She told me to buy a new suit for tomorrow and I totally forgot."

"Not a problem. We'll get it right now."

Invisible hands measured me, then immediately other hands started cutting out a pattern from the fabric I had selected.

"I never imagined this was even a thing," I admitted to the seamstress.

"We pride ourselves on the highest-quality daemonological tailoring in the Capital," she said with a grin. "Our turn-around time is an hour for most projects, and ten minutes for repairs and cleaning."

In other words, this had to cost an absurd amount.

On the other hand, I did have money for now.

For now.

"A walk?" Alice suggested.

"Sure?" I followed her out.

She slowed until we walked side-by-side. "Our mutual friend has no one to tell her no. And she doesn't like it when people tell her no. I certainly have to walk cautiously around her. And yet when *you* tell her no, she isn't angry."

"Like I said, I've never really seen her angry." Only at the chef who nearly poisoned her.

"I was at London when she destroyed it," Alice said matter-of-factly.

"The final stand of the Old Magisterium?"

"She leveled an entire city to destroy us. The daemon she manifested was so powerful that it ripped up the streets just from the gravitational pull. I remember the rain falling sideways. The Rank X crushed all those in the College itself in about a minute. Then we surrendered, before she let it rampage any further." Everything she said was in a level tone, but I saw the turmoil within her eyes.

"I'm sorry." Yet the Lynn I knew would laugh off any joke. Were we really talking about the same person?

"Darius told the survivors that cooperation was the least bad option left. So we did, at least a large chunk of us. Things were brutal for a few months. But although I sometimes wish things were different, the world is a little better under one ruler. And as long as that ruler is happy, the world is safe."

"I understand."

"Good. Then keep doing whatever you're doing." She looked around. "I might as well give you more information on her—things to look out for. Warning signs. Things she enjoys, and the things that will calm her down."

"I see. Yeah, tell me." If Lynn got angry, this would help.

And yet I didn't want to be Chief Emotional Bomb Squad Technician to the Crown.

I wanted to be her boyfriend.

The others in the Needle's Eye looked differently at me in my new suit: if not with respect, at least not contempt. Maybe all I needed was a change of clothes and confidence.

Lynn was as gorgeous as ever, in a completely different dress. She still wore the diamond moon necklace. "Let's see what we'll have this time. *Daisu o kudasai.*" She rolled the dice. "Huh. I've never had that. Let's see what it's like."

"Do you do this for fun or to avoid possible poisons?"

"Both," she said with a gleaming smile. "By the way, I like your suit. Where'd you get it?"

"Abigail's Daemonic Tailoring."

"Ah, Abigail's. I considered binding textile daemons, too, before I became the Imperatrix, but..." She glanced around her and fell silent.

Alice had told me Lynn didn't like to talk about the past. That was fine. I had my own past, if a less violent one. "Speaking of binding, I got one of those daemon-proof cellphones. They told me I need someone to bind some daemon to it or something."

"I will," Lynn said immediately. A waiter arrived with wine. I tested it; she drank. "To be clear: daemon-proof is not what you think it means. Technically they're called CBAS, COMP Ban Abiding Smartphones."

"What do I think it means? Wait, no," I held my head.

Lynn giggled. "What I mean is that it will detect another daemon messing with its electronics, but it can't stop a more powerful daemon. Of course at some level the more powerful daemon will just snap the phone in two, but you get what I mean?"

"I do."

"Also, if a file exists anywhere in the world—" Lynn said.

"Excuse me, Your Imperial Majesty," a thin man said, stepping beside us with a wineglass in hand. "I had an opportunity for both of us, and I was wondering whether we could discuss..." As the man rambled on, Lynn's eyes began to narrow. The thin man began gesturing more and more until the wine began sloshing. "Hold this, would you?"

I took the glass without thinking.

"*Kono jama o doukanasai. Yukkuri,*" Lynn murmured. Invisible hands picked up the thin man and slowly carried him away. Everyone else pointedly ignored his panicked shrieking on his journey to the other side of the room. The hands gently dropped him. "*Gurasu mo.*" The wine glass left my hands and landed by the man. He took it and fled the scene. "Where was I?"

Did Lynn just do that because she was annoyed, or because she didn't want any distractions from me? "Something about files?"

"Yes. If a file exists anywhere in the world, perhaps even one that has since been deleted, a sufficiently powerful daemon can know its contents, regardless of if it has access or not."

"What?"

"Daemonic knowledge. Usually only see it in Rank V and above. They just *know.*"

"That doesn't make sense." Maybe Kyle was right, and there really were daemons scraping the truth off the web.

"I know, right?" Lynn smiled. "It's one of the great mysteries of daemonology. Why do daemons just have knowledge, without learning it? Because of it, some people thought they're real demons, all the way back to their discovery on the Lunar Outpost."

"I'll have to ask Professor Jameson about it. But you don't think they're real demons?"

"I don't believe real demons exist, no. But even if they did, I've found most daemons have a strong sense of morality. Especially when they think you're in the wrong."

"Really?"

"Really."

"I didn't know they talked back."

"They rarely talk to people other than their masters." At that moment, some kind of dish arrived. "I can't read Traditional Chinese that well, but if I'm correct this is... fried chicken uterus."

"Well," I said. "It looks delicious, to be honest."

"I'm up for it."

"So am I. Lord, may this dish not be poisoned, even accidentally, whatever this is..."

I felt whatever anger or resentment I might have held at Lynn slowly fading away as we ate, talked, and laughed.

"By the way!" Lynn burst out. "I have a big surprise planned for you this Saturday."

"It's not a surprise if you tell me it's coming," I said.

"I'm not," she said with a smug grin. "I'm telling you that there *will* be a surprise, not what it is. But I'll give you a hint." She leaned in.

I leaned in, too.

"MC^2."

"Uh, OK?"

She sat back with her best mischievous expression.

"By the way, Lynn, I was wondering if I could watch you bind the daemon to my new phone."

"If you're that curious, yes, but it will be very boring to watch."

"No, really, I'm looking forward to it," I insisted.

"As long as you sit quietly and don't say anything." She looked elsewhere, as if reading invisible text. "I've got meetings for the next two hours, but after that, I'll just show up at your apartment. Sound like a plan?"

"Sounds like a plan."

I had not *trashed* the place, but I was a bachelor. I briefly panicked until I realized I could just...have someone clean it for me.

In fact, it was a magister, who stepped in the building for one minute, snapped her fingers and spoke in some language, then walked back out, leaving the place spotless behind her.

"Man." I plopped into my recliner. "If only—" Oh. Oh no. I *had* asked someone to serve me, hadn't I?

I had promised myself this would never go that far.

Whatever. It was hardly menial labor if you had daemons do the work for you, right?

The doorbell rang. I hurried to let Lynn inside.

"Welcome!" I greeted her. "...Are you all right?"

"Just a little tired," she said. She looked a lot more than a little tired. "Comes with the job. Anyway, where's your phone?"

"I just left it on the table."

"C'mon, you didn't even take it out of the box?"

"Well, I didn't know if I could do that yet."

"You'll get to a screen that tells when you need a magister. C'mon. Open it!"

I had never seen someone so happy to watch someone else open a box, but Lynn was grinning ear to ear. I savored the pristine black thing for a moment, then looked for the SIM card slot.

"Here, I brought a SIM card for you," she said.

"Sure thing," I said, and handed her my old SIM.

She snapped it in two.

I looked at her.

"Sorry!" she said brightly. "Habit."

"Where on Earth do you learn *that* habit?"

"Let's just say I changed phones a lot, once upon a time. Anyway, let me just insert it for you." She snapped her fingers and an invisible hand opened the phone and inserted the SIM card.

I turned on the phone and swiped through several screens. Then it came to a screen with nothing but sets of numbers. "What on Earth is this?" *Ask a magister to help you with this screen.*

"These are constructions." Lynn snapped her fingers and received paper, pencils, a protractor, and rulers. Invisible hands lifted the phone to her eye level as she rapidly drew a daemonic inscription on the paper. "This inner inscription matches the inscription on the phone's circuitry. They can't display it on the screen because there would be too many copies. Plus it would violate the COMP Ban."

"The what?"

She paused. "Because daemons can control computers, it's forbidden to make computers that can control daemons. All hell would break loose otherwise."

"Makes sense."

"Anyway, daemonic inscriptions are given as a list of geometry construction instructions. Or constructions, as they're commonly called. This outer inscription will attract daemons."

"Like fishing," I suggested.

"I've never gone fishing, actually. But this close to the Palace's gravity generators and they're all over the place. Now you'll have to shut up for a bit." Lynn started talking rapidly in Japanese and more sophisticated looking gear appeared. She placed the phone on the diagram and started clicking a device.

She was right about it being boring. I didn't see anything and she didn't talk out loud. I started wishing I knew Morse code. Still, what chance did most people have to see the Witch-Queen at work like this?

I watched the clock tick away. About ten minutes in, Lynn got up. Then swore. "Great, I didn't think to bring a chemical hood. Backup plan." She sat back down and clicked away again.

Five minutes later, she snapped her fingers again. A giant candle appeared, easily the size of the paschal candle at St. Malachi's, and lit itself on its own. "Just let this burn. I can't stay much longer, but you won't need to do anything. When it goes out, you can use your phone."

"I didn't know daemons like candles."

"This daemon likes calories. You wouldn't believe how much energy is in this candle. Anyway, got to go *now*. See you Saturday! *Ikimashou!*" She snapped her fingers and was gone.

I watched the candle burn. Strange how my hope felt like that: one small flame melting a whole pillar of my life.

6

Decadence

"**D**id you sort out things with your girlfriend?" Professor Jameson asked me with a teasing look.

"Oh. Sort of. It's complicated."

"It always is."

"Not to change the subject, but—she talked about daemonic knowledge."

"Ah, yes. I suppose we might as well get to that. But first, what do you think a daemon is?"

I shrugged. "I don't know. Some kind of spirit or energy being?"

"Those are mighty different categories."

"So they are. What do you think?"

"You have no idea how many times I get asked that. But it was my job after all." He leaned in. "A daemon is a person, a rational creature made in the image of God."

"Wow."

"Are they fallen? Possibly, but not as angels are. They seem able to choose both good and evil, like we do."

"So is it right to, er, bind them?"

The old professor shrugged. "They certainly seem willing enough to be bound. But so are some humans."

I fell silent.

"Before the Empire, I used to say 'freedom is in choosing which master to serve.' But that became a bit of an Imperial slogan, so I stopped."

"What... *do* you feel about the Empire?"

He raised a white eyebrow. "If you're wondering about my personal feelings on the subject, I don't see that they matter. If the pope's OK with it, I don't have any right to object."

"My dad had a hard time with it," I said. "I don't know."

"You might want to sort that out if you're dating the Imperatrix Mundi."

"It's easier to think of her as the Imperatrix when you're not right next to her," I said.

"You know, that's the first time anyone has ever said that to me."

"...Huh."

"You really do have feelings for her. Hold on to that. No matter what happens, you know at least your own feelings are authentic."

"I guess I do."

Saturday arrived, and as per Lynn's text I walked to one of the Palace landing pads in my new suit. I supposed it would be prudent to get another, just in case I needed a second in an emergency.

I shook myself as I approached the sleek black limo. I would need to know that Lynn wanted me back before I got used to this.

Or at least, knew she wanted me as I wanted her.

A servant in immaculate livery bowed and showed me inside. The interior was massive, at least wide enough to play ping-pong. I wouldn't have been surprised if it was one of the largest aircars in the world.

I sat and fidgeted. I didn't imagine this would be another restaurant, but Lynn certainly liked to eat. Maybe we were going somewhere *super* fancy.

"Boo!"

I spun to see Lynn grinning in a fabulous black gown. No skin showed above her high neckline, and she smelled of an exotic perfume. "Hey, Lynn. Where are we going?"

"Monte Carlo!"

"What?"

"The casino! They're having their yearly special event, Monte Carlo Mutant Chess. I've been looking forward to it for months."

"Uh... OK," I said. "I'm not really a fan of casinos." Not that I could ever have afforded to go to one.

"C'mon, you'll enjoy it." She snapped her fingers, and we lifted off.

"Is it a chess tournament?"

"More or less. Don't worry, it's super simple. And—oh, yeah, you haven't met my friends yet, have you?"

Lynn had *friends*? No one had ever mentioned such a concept before. But I supposed if I was actually being taken to meet them, I was being upgraded from mere anime-watching buddy at least. Whatever that made me. "I'll be interested to meet them," I said sincerely.

About half an hour of flight over the ocean later, Lynn chattering increasingly elatedly about Monte Carlo, we descended to another landing pad. A chauffeur opened the door, and we stepped out into sunlight and the smell of sea salt.

I didn't realize it, but the Monte Carlo Casino was a pretty huge place, overlooking the ocean. Fancy aircars were landing nearby, and I thought I spotted a Aerolls-Royce.

"Your Imperial Majesty," said a fat man in a suit, bowing nearly to the ground. I couldn't tell if he was a flunky or literally the boss, but Lynn seemed to know him. "Welcome. We've prepared a private section for you and your friends." He motioned to another man.

"Of course," Lynn said with a smile. "This way, Mike."

I expected contempt or disinterest from the fat guy as I passed, but I only saw curiosity. To be fair, I was pretty curious about it all, too.

Monte Carlo's interior was fancier than cathedrals I had visited or seen online. I couldn't even call it tasteless. No, everything was in perfect shape and high quality, even diamond-studded chandeliers. I watched Lynn's eyes move around the place with pleasure, as if she had finally found a place fit for her.

No, no, that wasn't it at all. It was as if this was a playground she had always wanted to go to as a kid, and now she had a chance.

We came to the private section, and behold, rich young men and women, all in their twenties. They immediately got up and knelt at her entrance. "At ease," Lynn waved a hand. "Everyone, this is Michael Mason. Mike, this is... everyone."

I didn't know how I could learn the names of all of Lynn's "friends," though I immediately ascertained that scare quotes were necessary. First off, the place was crammed with non-rich people: flunkies, guards in suits and sunglasses, and arm candy fawning over their owners. I couldn't object to the arm candy, given as I might technically fall into that category. But the real deal, by the calm looks in their eyes, had immediately started to analyze how much influence I had over Lynn, and how they could get influence over me.

Was Lynn delusional? Surely she knew these people were only in it because she was the Witch-Queen. Or did she know and not care?

Whatever. I wasn't going to judge her life choices. "Hello, everyone," I said awkwardly.

"Here," Lynn snapped her fingers, and a throne appeared, with another chair by her right hand. She sat in the throne. I sat beside her.

Their eyes changed in an instant: as if we had been friends for life.

No, Lynn knew. She knew that she had invited a sheep to a dinner with her fellow wolves. And she knew those same wolves would eat her alive if it gave them what they wanted.

"Your Imperial Majesty," a thin young man in glasses, with a girl behind him pretending she was interested in nerds, raised a booklet. "I'm curious about your feelings on the latest rule changes."

"I haven't actually followed them, Albert," Lynn said. "I like to keep an element of surprise."

I could sense the slightest tension shift in the group, as if wondering if she was going to attack the rich nerd. But he simply nodded gently, as if the comment was his own idea, and the tension dissipated.

"I, for one, am glad they are finally removing the teleporting queen from that stupid army," another rich young man said. "Which one was it?" he asked his flunky.

"The Teleporting Terminators, Your Highness," the flunky said.

Your *Highness*? Suddenly, it all made sense. Of all two hundred dominions in the world, these were the royals young enough to potentially be Lynn's peers. And being her friend would practically be mandatory.

And that also explained why none of them dressed like magisters—an expression of the infamous separation of magic and nobility that Lynn insisted for everyone but herself.

But I kept my thoughts to myself. Lynn would probably protect me, but I didn't want to tick off anyone here, either. I was just the arm candy.

Right?

"They can't call them the Teleporting Terminators if they don't all teleport," an Asian, and somewhat fat, princess said languidly.

"It needs to alliterate, Chen," a prince told her.

"They aren't terminating now, without their stupid overpowered queen."

"Let's see how they do this round, then," Lynn said.

Nods followed, of course.

Men in suits wheeled a cart full of liquor bottles into the room. I wondered if the total cost of the booze amounted to a figure in the millions.

"Now for the most important roll of the day, of course," another prince said.

"Ah, you flatter me," Lynn said. "*Daisu o kudasai.*" Dice appeared in her hand, and she rolled on the floor. "Cognac." She snapped her fingers and the dice returned to her hands. She rolled a few more times. "I don't think I've ever had that."

"Oh, it's a treat," Chen told her. "Especially with the 2070 Champagne..."

I was trying to keep my composure at being with people who had fancy booze so often they had opinions on it. God help us if they started talking about bouquets next.

"You know, why not? Cocktails tonight!"

The bartender nodded and began pouring from bottle after bottle. Making a cocktail from mixing several bottles of the same alcohol probably committed some kind of booze-sin, but it was inevitable considering Lynn's precautions.

She snapped her fingers and long-stemmed glasses flew to each of us.

"To a quality time tonight!" Lynn raised her glass.

"To tonight!" her friends replied, and sipped. I paused, then realized they were all staring at me.

Of course, the one who doesn't drink the booze is the one who poisoned it. I sipped and almost spat out the burning, fuzzy drink. Holy *cow* that was a lot of alcohol. I resolved to toss it down the drain at my first opportunity.

Lynn, seeing no one obviously dying, sipped. "Ah, I can see your point," she said to the princess. She turned to an attendant. "When *is* the tournament starting?"

"In two hours, Your Imperial Majesty."

"No need to waste the time, then," Lynn said. "Bring us a blackjack table, would you?"

"Of course."

"Raphael, how is that museum of yours coming?" Albert asked the prince who had been complaining about the Terminators.

"I can't get it started with all the protests," he said. "I'm considering invoking eminent domain."

"No," Lynn said sharply.

The room froze.

"I'll think of something," Raphael said.

"Toss them something," Chen suggested. "Or lower a tax. Works like a charm."

"Speaking of taxes, I was wondering if we could get that trade deal..." another prince said.

My head spun. Of course. This was a meeting of some of the most powerful and rich people in the world. Decisions that would affect entire dominions were idle chatter while waiting for a blackjack table.

This might be *Lynn's* idea of a good time, but I realized it was my own idea of a private hell. But hey, why not enjoy it for what it was? I sipped the cocktail and almost spat the stuff out again.

The table, numerous chairs, a dealer, and a woman magister with a card reader and a cart full of chips and plaques arrived. The latter moved around the room, helping people in-debt themselves so they could gamble. Chips and plaques flew as the royalty handed play money to their pets.

Lynn gave me a pile of plaques. "Just bet with me," she whispered in my ear. "Uh, OK," I whispered back.

Most of the group went to the table, everyone but me giving Lynn a fair bit of space. I knew how to play blackjack, but I followed Lynn's instructions. Each seat at the table held three sets of betting circles, which would share the same fate as one player. The arm candy bet with their owners. I placed a plaque and tried to ignore that the lowest number was 10,000. The dealer dealt, and we were off.

We won the first hand. My adrenaline spiked, but I forced myself to concentrate. We lost the next two. I felt unsteady, as if reality was unraveling before me.

Lynn watched everything with intent eyes, and she looked both too focused and too smug. She bet small at first, then suddenly began betting big. If Lynn wasn't card counting, I didn't know Lynn.

What did that make me? A gambling cheat by proxy? Lynn was betting enormous sums of money even when she lost, and I was lost at all the hand motions and also losing my mind. But what could I do?

Inspiration struck.

"Hey, do you know where the bathrooms are?" I asked.

"I can take you there," an attendant said.

"Don't let go of your drink," Lynn said, without turning from the cards. "And save some money for the main event!"

"I'll be careful," I promised. Then I scooped my wages of someone else's inquity and casually got the hell out of there.

"You've got taste, Lynn," I overheard Chen say as I stepped out of the room.

"Would you dump this?" I asked an attendant, who nodded solemnly. I handed off the booze with relief and went inside the fancy restroom.

It was spotless, but Monte Carlo had too much taste for gold-plated toilets. A guy did stand by the paper towel dispenser, and would presumably pull one for me, presumably for a tip.

What on Earth was I doing here? It made Lynn happy, and I supposed any relationship involved sacrifices.

"C'mon, though," I said to myself as I washed my hands, ignoring Paper Towel Guy. "Why not have some fun? Lynn sure is."

I walked out and stopped in thought. I could gamble at some other game. I had never gambled for more than Oreos before this, and I had no idea how to start. Or if I would stop.

"Michael, is it?" I spun to see a blond young man with sharp features and attentive blue eyes. He was one of the most handsome men I had ever seen, and wore a spotless suit. "Prince Frederik of the Scandinavian Dominion."

Oh, yeah, him. One of the old nobility that the Witch-Queen had arbitrarily decided to leave in power, maybe because of Denmark's unsuccessful clashes with its magisterium before Lynn destroyed them all. "I go by Mike, Your...er..."

"Oh, enough of that," he waved the title away. "We are all close friends of Lynn."

"I see that. I... uh, am looking for another game."

"Ah. Perhaps you're wondering if Her Imperial Majesty is, shall we say, advantage gambling?"

"Well, yes."

"Everyone knows it," he confided. "But her patronage is worth far more than however much she wins, and besides, she gambles on other games. Perhaps you would enjoy one of them instead?"

"Sure." There we go. I would gamble on some other game, which *did* have a house edge, and balance would be restored. "Do they have baccarat here?" I asked. I didn't care what the game was, but after seeing it in vintage James Bond films I had always been a little curious.

"Oh, most certainly. This way." He led me through the gilded hallways, past the noise of the slot machines, to a busy room with tables.

"How do I play?" The crowd of rich muckety-mucks instantly melted so I would have a prime seat.

"There's no need to worry about that," he said. "You'll see."

I saw, indeed. An accountant had once told me that gambling was an elaborate ritual to disguise the transfer of money. As much as I knew that, I couldn't help but notice my adrenaline climbing with the thrill of the game. I couldn't understand either the rules or people's tipsy explanations of them. James Bond's favorite game turned out to be something like blackjack, except there was only one hand, and the "house" was also a player, and no one could make any decisions, or... something? I couldn't follow it.

No difference from playing with Lynn, then, right?

The players cheered as they won. Someone tipped the dealer an obscene sum.

I looked through my plaques, couldn't tell how much I had started with or how much Lynn had won for me, then just bet a pile. My adrenaline surged, heart pumping as if against a primal threat.

The dealer dealt the cards. The "house" swore. We, the players, cheered.

I knew that the entire environment of the casino was there to make me make irrational decisions. I knew that the gambler's fallacy was a fallacy, and there was no way the casino was giving away money, however the hell the game worked. But as the dealer shuffled plaques my way, I felt more pleasure and a bigger rush in that one moment than I had ever felt playing a video game or any other form of entertainment. In one moment I was—200,000 IM richer.

I would keep winning, right? Just play another hand.

Dear God, I would get addicted to this, wouldn't I?

Maybe I should come here more often.

No. Time to stop while I was ahead. I pocketed the plaques and pulled myself away from the table.

"Baccarat not to your taste?" Prince Frederik asked.

"I, uh, yeah. Fun, though." I could swear I felt my voice shaking a little. "Looks pretty simple, really."

"Perhaps you'd enjoy something more intellectually stimulating, then? This is the championship day."

"The chess tournament thing, right?" I asked as we walked together.

"Of course. Monte Carlo likes to do everything differently, and this is an apt example."

I found myself in a room full of oversized chess boards on green felt, surrounded by magisters silently eying each other. Setting up for the tournament? Gilt and exquisitely carved as the foot-tall pieces were, they were not even normal chessmen.

Well, one set was. But every other set were strange shapes: polyhedra, gnomes, ones where all the pieces had heads like knights or turrets like rooks. When I spotted the fungi, I just had to look closer.

And look! They weren't just random cartoons, but sophisticated replicas of real mushrooms. The pawns were *Morchella eschulenta*, and the queen was an *Amanita phalloides,* the infamous death cap.

"I'm curious what brings you to these," Frederik said.

"I'm a fan of mushrooms."

"They are certainly new this round."

"I actually have no idea what the hell any of this is."

"This is one of the 64 armies tonight." He motioned to the chess pieces. "Each will play against the other armies. We place various bets on how they will do in the tournament. Each army is somewhat different, of course, but you can read about them on the felt."

I bent over and read the small text. The Furious Fungi, as they were called, had a variety of moves and powers, and although their pieces were weaker they could decompose captured pieces to plant new spores on the board. Kind of like the Japanese game *shogi*, except more...fungal. "Are they sure this is balanced?"

"They run millions of games by powerful computers, which, as I understand it, are deliberately hobbled to play at the skill of daemons."

"And daemons actually play in the tournament?"

"That is correct."

"So the teams are completely automated."

"That is also correct."

Now I got it. This was an autobattler for rich people too cultured to admit they played video games.

"Pardon me if I ask a personal question," Frederik said. "You see, Lynn is known for sudden mood shifts. It is in all of our best interests if we know what she wants, you see."

"What?"

He dropped to a whisper. "How long have you known her?"

"Just a few months," I said, feeling the heat rise in my face. "Why?"

"Ah. I was wondering how... well, close you were."

"We're plenty close," I snapped.

"Good, then." He looked around. "You are certainly different from all her previous Companions. The previous ones were so... straight-laced. Perhaps you're different."

I wanted to punch him, but decided to read the felt some more rather than deign to acknowledge him. The magister by the table watched us with concern. "Are these the odds?" I asked her deliberately, tapping on a grid beside the special rules.

"Those are relative wins and losses during the simulations. The actual betting is parimutuel."

"Fascinating." I didn't have a clue what the hell parimutuel betting even was, but I'd be damned if I asked while Mr. Royal Asshole was there. I dug out my plaques. I'd be even more damned if I didn't bet on the fungi. Even if they had a bad batting average. "How do we bet?"

"Just place your bet on the felt."

"Where's 'will win the tournament'?"

"Over here." The place was labeled WIN. Simple enough, I supposed.

I dumped all my markers on WIN and invisible hands took it away. There. I would be done after this, no matter what happened.

The magister's eyes widened a little.

What the hell had I done? I thought the next moment. That had been... around 500,000 IM?

"Excuse me," I said to no one in particular, and hurried off.

I breathed in the sea salt and tried to clear my mind.

It wasn't my money. Lynn had bought those plaques for me, and then cheated to get more, and then OK so I won at baccarat but she provided the initial money...

I had still potentially thrown away half a million IM in one bet.

What had my life become?

Could I ever go back?

Did I even want to go back?

I breathed deeply. And breathed again. My heart still pulsed like I was on a hunt, overwhelming me.

"Mike?" came Lynn's voice. I swiveled around to see her with a concern on her face. "Where were you? The tournament's about to start."

"I just... this place isn't for me."

"Aw. We can leave right after the tournament. Promise."

"Sure," I said, and followed her back in.

"Ladies and gentlemen, we welcome all of you to tonight's special, Monte Carlo Mutant Chess!" proclaimed the fat man from before. The crowd cheered from its position in the balcony, and I found myself among them. "As usual, this will be six rounds of Swiss, followed by the top eight advancing to an elimination bracket. In five minutes we'll start, so place your final bets now!"

"I don't get why you always bet on the Fabulous FIDEs," Chen said to Albert.

"They calibrate all the other armies to be approximately as strong as them," Albert replied. "So I note they have consistently performed."

"What did you bet on?" Lynn asked me.

"I went all in on the mushrooms."

"Ha!" she laughed. "Knew it."

Maybe it was proximity and maybe it was the environment, but I could really smell Lynn's perfume now.

"What did you bet on?" I asked her.

"A little bit of everything. I just like to watch, really."

That seemed remarkably unlike Lynn, but who was I to argue?

"Place your final bets!" the announcer said. Gamblers hurried around the room below. "Five, four—"

"—Three, two, one!" we chanted.

"Let the games begin!"

An orchestra began playing over the loudspeakers. Magisters all over the floor below chanted, clapped, or snapped fingers. The pieces all flew into the air and arranged themselves against their random match.

"Let's see if the Teleporting Terminators've still got it," a princess said.

"I hope so, because if they bring back that goddamn teleporting queen—" Raphael started.

I ignored the chatter and watched the mushrooms. *My* mushrooms. I could see why they hadn't done so well in simulations. The other army was full of dragons, and the enemy daemon kept its pieces well at a distance and attacked without actually moving to capture. We lost the first game, won the second, then lost the third.

But this was Swiss, so they'd play several more rounds. Besides, I told myself, I was having fun on Lynn's dime. The money didn't matter at this point.

Right?

Soon enough my intuition proved correct. If the other army lost even a few pieces, our fungal self-replication replenished our own army, until the overwhelming mass of mushrooms mated their king.

"Told you!" Raphael said. The Teleporting Terminators were fourth place.

"Maybe the Terrible Terminators?" someone suggested.

"Terrible? They're doing great!"

I watched the standings carefully. The Seeping Switchers lost to the Fabulous FIDEs, putting the latter in the Top 8. Albert and his erstwhile paramour rejoiced. Meanwhile, the Furious Fungi beat out the Colorbound Clobberers to also break into the Top 8.

Lynn let out a bit of a girly squeal. "Look, Mike!"

"I see it!" What if I actually *won?*

Magisters hurried off the defeated armies. I saw some of them look dejected—perhaps they would have been paid more if their daemons had won. Chips and plaques flew up and landed by some of Lynn's coterie and among the rest of the crowd.

Albert was covered with chips and plaques.

"Oh Jesus, you bet it all on Place bets again, didn't you?" Raphael demanded.

"I have a system," Albert insisted.

"This is Monte Carlo. There is no system."

"This is Mutant Chess. There very much is."

"He's told me all about it," Albert's arm candy said, and kissed him on the cheek. He stroked her hair.

"And we're off to the final battles!" the announcer said.

The pieces played slower. The chatter dissipated, as we held our breaths at each capture. Prince Frederik took a seat by me and Lynn. "Your Majesty." He genuflected. "I see your Companion chose wisely."

"I didn't bet on the mushrooms at all," Lynn said. "But Mike's into mushrooms."

"I am," I admitted. *Because unlike you, I had to scrounge for a living,* I managed not to say.

Our enemy in the first round was the Bearish Bulls, a stock market-themed army that advanced in jagged lines and could purchase more pieces. I wondered how they would do against us, as the more pieces they purchased, and we captured, the more pieces we would have.

I didn't need to worry. The Furious Fungi so crushed them that one of their unfortunate "investors" slammed his fist against the railing. Chips flew into a giant pile—the losing bets, presumably.

Next up we faced the Fabulous FIDEs. I had tried to figure out their gimmick, until I realized there was no gimmick: it was simply a standard chess set. They won the first game, but we won the next two.

I felt more heady, as if I had drunk more than I thought. "Looks like we're—you're winning!" Lynn said. Then I felt even *more* heady.

We fought the semifinals against the Maharajah's Men, an especially weird army with one super-piece and a bit of cannon fodder. But our army's daemon had some sense, and advanced slowly, eventually neutralizing the Maharajah with precisely placed pieces. We won 2-0.

A dark-skinned princess in a sari sighed. "Never bet on your home team."

"It's working well for Mike," Lynn said.

"And now for the final battle, the upstart Furious Fungi against the old favorites, the Teleporting Terminators!"

"Who here bet on the Terminators?" Lynn asked.

Frederik raised his hand, as did a few others.

"They need to nerf them some more," Raphael sighed.

I watched the pieces as if I could affect the outcome. Please, God. Let me kick his ass.

"How much did you bet, anyway?" Lynn asked me.

"Like... 500,000 IM."

The whole balcony turned to look at me.

"How much do I stand to win?" I asked.

"It's parimutuel," Albert explained. "If the Fungi win, you split all opposing bets relative to the size of your own."

Oh. *Oh.*

"Let me find out," Lynn motioned to an attendant and whispered in his ear. He nodded and hurried off.

I could see why the Teleporting Terminators had done so well. They could teleport through other armies' pieces, although not to capture. A wall of pawns meant nothing to them.

But it also meant that our army had more to snack on. Game One was hotly contested, but ended in victory for them.

Please, God. I don't care about the money. I just want to win.

What the hell was I even thinking?

Game two, the Terminators' daemon made a serious blunder and lost their queen. We won.

The whole balcony fell into a deep silence.

The attendant returned. "You'll win 1.4 million IM," Lynn said matter-of-factly. "*If* you win."

Game three, I watched as the battle went back and forth. The Terminators took many pieces at the beginning, but lost enough that our side could regenerate from their corpses. The clocks ticked down. The daemons slowed all the more, thinking through their moves.

I almost started to pray again, but stopped myself. It was only a game, right?

Then the pieces hurried in movement, the sign that one side had found a checkmate. Seven moves later, and we had won.

"Victory to the Furious Fungi! What an upset!"

The whole crowd roared. Lynn jumped up and cheered. I jumped up and cheered with her. Plaques flew up and rained on me.

"One point four million imperial marks," Lynn said, grinning ear to ear. "All yours."

"All mine," I said in a daze. *YES!*

"Congratulations, Mike!" cheered someone.

"You did it!"

"Go Fungi!" Raphael said.

I looked at Lynn, and her gleaming smile was the most beautiful thing in the world. I could have lived forever in that moment, looking at nothing else.

I leaned over and kissed her.

She froze, then shoved me back with more force than being tackled by a linebacker. Before I could even think or apologize, she shrieked and ran off.

Dear God, what have I done?

7

Consequences

Lynn's friends all stared at me. Albert's arm candy met my eyes with a bit of a shrug. Rafael watched me with curiosity. Chen looked disappointed.

I tore away from them to see the smirking Scandinavian prince.

"Perhaps she's so not into you after all," he said.

"Keep your goddamn mouth to yourself," I snapped.

"Oh, but isn't that what you just didn't do?"

In one step I was next to him. In the next I cracked my fist against his face.

He staggered back with a bloody mouth. My own fist hurt like hell.

Jacked magisters phased in immediately.

"Ethect him!" the prince said. He spit out a bloody tooth.

The muscle grabbed me. "This way, sir."

"Hey, hey, I'll come quietly," I told them.

Everything was fancy in Monaco, including the jail. It stood tall on a craggy cliff by the sea. They probably had diamond-studded toilets, part of my mind noted absently.

The rest of my mind was replaying the incident over and over again, in slow motion.

What the hell had I done?

Was Lynn germophobic? Did she not like kissing?

Did she not like *me*?

The pit in the bottom of my stomach opened to an abyss. What if—what if this was the end? What if it had always been a game to her, and now she was done playing?

But no, hadn't she gone above and beyond with me? Didn't she like me more than all the rest of her Companions? Right? *Right?*

And screw that royal bastard. The pain in my hand was still worth it. He had set me up, hadn't he? Egging me on to touch Lynn or—

Or... maybe Lynn was just sensitive to touch. Maybe that was all.

The guard post let us in. I sighed. Off to the drunk tank.

The drunk tank turned out to be the one thing in Monaco that *wasn't* fancy. Figured. Although my only prior experience with jail had been visiting Dad, the place looked like any other drunk tank, complete with way too many people. Two apparent prostitutes, a drunken businessman singing off-key, two gangsters glaring at each other, one mobster looking around calmly, a very, very angry American in a suit bellowing oaths at everyone, and several others who looked around in fear and/or inebriation.

The door shut behind me. I found a place to sit.

I hadn't even noticed the indignity of it. And they were probably going to search me at some point. But all I cared about was one thing:

I couldn't contact Lynn.

I had been told that their phone system had suddenly stopped working, just as I arrived. What in God's name? But they didn't let me argue, just shuffling me off over here, where—

"You! You're the Companion, aren't you?"

Dear please God no.

The angry businessman got up and stomped over to him. "Jesus Christ this is all your fault. Your goddamn girlfriend ruined my casino!"

"You own Monte Carlo Casino?" I asked.

"No, you asshole. The Five-of-a-Kind, in Las Vegas!"

The Five-of-the-Kind? Where Lynn's killer daemons had disobeyed her? I opened my mouth to argue that it wasn't her fault, but—Lynn had told me the story secretly.

Lynn.

My heart twisted.

My lack of reply only made him angrier. "She almost leveled the place! She killed hundreds! And then when she became Ms. Bitch-Queen she threw it all down the memory hole—"

"Shut your goddamn mouth!" I yelled.

"Quiet!" a guard ordered.

We all fell silent, except for the drunk, who was still merrily singing.

"Hey, she like girls, too?" one of the prostitutes asked. "We could—"

"Just leave me the hell alone," I said.

They all did.

Time passed. Without a clock, I had no way of knowing if it was hours or minutes. "Each day in here is like a year / a year whose days are long," to quote Oscar Wilde. Without external events to date the present moment, every minute felt longer than the previous one.

And over and over again I thought through it in my mind.

What had I done?

Had Lynn been touched inappropriately before?

Was she not ready?

Did she not like me back?

I felt sick. If only I had had a chance to call or even text her. I could smooth things over...

Unless, the voice whispered in my mind, there is no smoothing over. Maybe this is the end.

Like Lexi and Emily and Amanda and Samantha and—OK, not Samantha, because she had ghosted me.

But *why*, God? I mouthed. What the hell did I do to *you*? Why the hell am I struggling finding a girlfriend, and the one time I don't even try, I end up with someone I like, and—

Did my suffering even matter to you, God? Were you tormenting me because I wasn't worthy? Or because you got off on my pain? Didn't you have anything better to do than make your own creatures suffer?

The walls of the cell vibrated a little, then a loud siren went off.

The drunk guy sobered instantly. The mobster swore in French.

"What's going on?"

"Something big is *hic* manifestin' *hic*," the drunk managed.

"Yeah, this is exactly what a daemonic battle feels like before it goes down," the mobster said.

Jesus Christ—like, literally, Jesus Christ, never mind, man, I didn't mean—

Unless this was Lynn.

A guard rushed in. "Michael Mason?"

I got up.

"Please come with me, sir."

I saw Lynn's daemons before I saw her. I'd only seen high-ranking daemons on TV before, but even at night I recognized the hazy shapes in the air and surrounding her. Beside her stood a tall figure like a knight, bending the light bluish around it.

She sat on a crude throne on a pile of rubble with legs, which stood some distance beyond the gate. Magisters stood around on the ground below, with edges in their expression.

I approached. "Lynn?" I called.

"Mike!" Lynn cried. "Hold still!"

I did, and the road beneath me tore itself off and brought me atop the rubble-thing.

Lynn looked a true Witch-Queen, edged fury in her eyes. "Are you all right? Did they hurt you? What's going on?"

"I... I just punched someone," I said. "They stuck me in the drunk tank. That's all."

Lynn's face went through several thoughts in a moment, arriving in a decision the next instant. "Stand down!" she ordered. She snapped her fingers and the daemons disappeared. She got up and moved almost to hug me and stopped herself. "I was so worried!"

This—this wasn't the look of a woman who was done playing with a plaything. This was the look of a woman who had almost lost a loved one. "Why the big welcome?" I asked.

"You didn't call! I thought you were angry, so I didn't call either," Lynn said. "But then hours passed, and so I wondered if you were all right. I phased over here to see the city in an uproar. Someone was daemonically jamming the telephony system here."

"Oh. Yeah. They said the phones weren't working."

"Don't be so *calm* about it, you big dummy! What if an assassin had come? What if—" She took a deep breath. "You're safe now. That's what matters."

She walked over to the edge. "Just stay here until the SMP arrives," she called. "I'll pay you all overtime. I want to know who did this!"

Lynn snapped her fingers, and the rubble lowered itself to the ground. "Just wait. The limo will be here eventually. And don't worry about the PR. I already have a delay on reports for you. It'll all get sorted."

"Thanks..."

The limo arrived and we hurried inside. I took a deep breath. Lynn snapped her fingers and we took off.

"What the hell did I do?" I asked.

"I'm... I'm very sensitive to touch," Lynn said. "That was the first time anyone had touched me, let alone *kissed* me, for three years. I... I wasn't ready." She looked me in the eyes. "Mike, I have boundaries. And that really, really crossed them."

"I'm sorry, I—" I had, what, been too excited? Egged on by that jerk? Wondering the truth? Because she had smiled? "I have no excuse. I'm sorry."

Lynn smiled and waved it away. "I'm feeling better now. But listen, Mike: I have upwards of forty protective daemons watching me on my time. If I hadn't shoved you away, they could have killed you."

"*What the hell?*"

Lynn looked at me. "What?"

"You have something so dangerous, and you don't even tell anyone?"

"I put it in the employee manual. If no one touches me, it's no big deal."

"What if it goes off by accident?"

She didn't say anything. She didn't even look at me.

I waited.

She still didn't answer.

Maybe it would be better to change the subject. "Lynn, what are we? Was this only a game? Or..."

"This... This was real," Lynn said. "You really are special to me. But." She looked at me with pain. "But I was playing around. I didn't want to commit. I just wanted to have fun. I'm sorry."

I wanted to touch her hand. "I... I accept your apology."

"Do you still want this?" Lynn asked. "Even after all I've done? I can get Lumberton sorted and send you back, if you want. I can—"

"Lynn, I want to be with you."

Lynn breathed. "Perfect. Let's make it official, then." Before I knew it her soft velvet gloves were on my face and she was leaning and her mouth was open and—

And we kissed.

My spirit soared within me, my whole body responding at once to her honest touch. Her lips were cool, but as if I could warm her with my entire passionate soul I pulled her in. She made a kind of moan and kissed me harder.

Then she pulled away, looking a bit tipsy. "That. That was worth being touched for."

"You can have seconds if you'd like," I replied, a little tipsy myself.

"Oh yes." She leaned in again.

My bones shuddered no less the second time. I stroked her hair and felt the hardness of the Imperial Diadem.

Who cared if she was the Witch-Queen? She was Lynn.

We broke off. "Does your daemonic protection cool down?" I asked.

"I have a warning if it's too much," Lynn said.

And we kissed again.

We made out for the rest of the trip home.

8

The Witch-Boyfriend

We kissed outside my apartment. Lynn gently ran a hand through my hair. "I'll see you tomorrow," she said. "Assuming no big crisis. But I'll definitely stop by for a moment if that's all I can do."

I squeezed her hand. "That's enough."

Lynn smiled wider and kissed me on the cheek. "Tomorrow. We'll have most of the day off."

"Tomorrow," I agreed. Then I saw the tears in her eyes. "Lynn? You're crying."

"I haven't been this happy in nine years, dear. One more." We kissed goodbye. "See ya! *Ikimashou.*" She snapped her fingers and was gone.

I walked inside and sat in my recliner. It was midnight, but I didn't feel sleepy in the slightest. Not only had I never been this happy in nine years, I had never been this happy before at all.

"Thanks, God," I said out loud. "I... I don't deserve this."

Should I pray more? Take up the cup of salvation and call on the name of the Lord? Nothing I could do seemed equal to the gift God had given me in Lynn.

I needed to tell everyone. But I probably should avoid making the news until Lynn was ready. She probably wanted to announce it publicly.

I sat back, and the only thing I could think of was Lynn's overjoyed smile. The smell of her perfume. Her kisses.

You know, I really should pray for her, that was what I should do. I got out my rosary and crossed myself with the crucifix.

The next morning, I was no less happy. I was still grinning ear-to-ear as I walked to Sunday Mass. I arrived early enough for confession, and found myself grinning even as I waited.

"Bless me, Father, for I have sinned," I said in the darkness, when it was my turn. "It's been two days, I think. I took the name of the Lord in vain twice, I punched an asshole in the face and, like, seriously injured him, and I crossed my girlfriend's boundaries and really hurt her feelings. But we reconciled! And, um, I sort of cheated at gambling. By proxy."

There was silence on the other end for a moment. "You did this all in two days?"

"It was a very busy night."

"I see. And you, to be clear, assaulted someone?"

"He was an asshole."

"I hear that. But you could get in serious legal trouble. Are you?"

"I, uh, got out of it. My girlfriend's... well-connected."

"You still need to apologize, donkey-pit or not."

"Sorry."

"Not to *me.*"

I sighed. "I'll send him a letter. Or I'll say something if I see him in person."

"Make the effort. Anything else?"

"In that... very busy night, I won a huge amount of money. And, well, I came in earlier with struggles with money. Also..." I paused. "See, I sort of won part of the money with my girlfriend's cheating."

"How on Earth do you cheat by proxy?"

"She was card counting and I was betting with her."

"Do you *know* she was card counting?"

"I mean, Lynn was—Oh God, I didn't just say that."

"You're safe. I'll die before telling anyone you're here."

"Thanks," I said. "I *think* she was card counting. She looked too smug about it."

"But do you know?"

"She implied it, at least."

"The reason I ask is that assuming someone is a gambling cheat is a form of rash judgment. Which you should definitely not do to your girlfriend, no matter her rank."

"I understand."

"But if you still feel guilty about the money, why not give it away? Or give some of it away? God gives us material wealth in order that we might gain eternal wealth by helping those in need. Even if this mammon is more iniquitous than others, you can still do just that."

"Yes, Father."

"Anything else?"

"That's all I can think of."

"For your penance, say a rosary for your girlfriend. And I'd advise you to keep up the practice regularly for the rest of your relationship, especially if you start moving towards a big commitment."

"All right."

"Now make your Act of Contrition."

"Oh my God, I am heartily sorry..."

That Mass, I could understand how happy Christ was for me to receive his whole self, when I was happy to even touch Lynn. "I'll love you first," I whispered. "But let me love Lynn second."

The moment I stepped outside I saw Lynn waiting for me in a kind of bubble of traffic. The other Mass-goers looked on her with fear, respect, or awe. To me, she just looked adorable in a dress I hadn't seen before.

"Lynn," I said, walking up to her and kissing her on the cheek. "If you wanted to come in…"

She responded by kissing me on the lips. "It'd be awkward. I've only been in a church once before, in my memory." She took my hand and tugged me. "Come along, we've got to keep moving."

"Why?"

"I swear, the paparazzi has a spy apparatus rivaling the SMP," she said with a smile. "If I stay in one place for more than a few minutes, they show up in force."

And of course they would eat this up. I walked along, even as Lynn gave my hand a squeeze and let go. "You've only been in a church once before?" I asked.

"Well, I was at the opening of the Basilica, too. But before that, I was hiding from the Magisterium. For whatever reason, the doors were unlocked, but no one was inside."

"That's usually how Catholic churches are."

"Huh. Anyway, when the Magisterium left, I snuck back out. Bad move. They had actually left an ambush. Wrecked the place." Lynn said it with a note of barely suppressed fury.

Numerous famous churches had been leveled when the Witch-Queen came to power, including the Cathedral of Notre Dame in Paris. She denied some of them, saying they were done by the Old Magisterium. But Lynn sounded so angry at this incident that I wondered what the truth was. "The Old Magisterium didn't care about religion," I ventured.

"The only thing the Old Magisterium cared about was itself," Lynn spat, then shook her head. "Let's talk about something else."

"Let's," I said.

All around us, traffic broke up to give us a wide berth. I saw every look from fear to excitement, hatred to love, not only at Lynn, but also at me.

I supposed this was the price of a real relationship with Lynn: if she was the Witch-Queen, I had just become the Witch-Boyfriend. But it all seemed worth it to see her smile at me like that.

"Are we going to have an official announcement?" I asked.

"There's no avoiding it. The best way to quash rumors about negative events is to start new rumors." She winked at me.

I didn't quite agree with that idea, but I smiled back anyway. "What now?"

"I don't know. We have basically all of today, and I've already scheduled the announcement for 3 PM. We should have lunch. Where to?"

"Huh?" I asked.

"C'mon, I've picked everywhere we've eaten so far. You pick somewhere."

We passed by a DaemonBurgers. "Here," I said.

"Perfect!"

I walked up to the glass door and opened it. Lynn stood out there for a moment, snapping her fingers a few times. "Well?" I asked.

"Checking it out," she said. "The counter-revolution will blow up anything and kill anyone."

"...Right," I said, a little nervous.

She smiled. "All good." She waltzed in with an amused glance.

Inside was almost spotless. The tables were clean, and one was being polished by a floating white towel. A lengthy line of customers snaked before the counters. The air smelled of way too much carbs and fat, and rang with murmurs and beeps. Invisible hands flipped burgers, fried fries, and poured drinks. A human cashier stood bored at the register. The only other human employee was a manager, looking around for any crisis the daemons couldn't handle.

Such, as, say, Her Imperial Majesty showing up. "It's her!" someone squealed, and the whole restaurant fell to their knees with the crashing of chairs.

Once again, I saw a little fear, but a good deal of them looked on us with excitement.

"At ease," Lynn said. They got up and began talking rapidly, glancing at us now and then. She walked up to the manager. "Give us the next ten orders. I'll pay for new ones."

"Of—of course, Your Imperial Majesty," the manager stammered, and began muttering in what sounded like Chinese.

"You can take mine, Your Imperial Majesty!" the girl in front said.

"Thank you," Lynn said.

The girl started cheerfully babbling.

Invisible hands brought brown bags to us. A little boy started crying, and the tall man with him picked him up and brought him before us. He knelt. "Please, Your Imperial Majesty!"

"Yes?" Lynn asked.

"That's the last green DevilRanger. We've looked all over the city..."

She unwrapped the bag, whispering in Japanese. An invisible hand took out the shrink-wrapped toy and gently carried it to the child. He looked up with tear-filled eyes and filled them with wonder. "Go on," she said. "Take it. It's safe."

The child snatched it and clutched it to himself.

"Say, 'Thank you, Your Imperial Majesty,'" I told him.

"Tank you, your impewial magesty."

"Close enough." Lynn smiled, and we left the two behind.

We sat at the farthest table from anyone else, one by the door. Lynn set out the food and I prayed. Then she rolled two ten-sided dice. "We'll split these two," she said.

I bit into a burger. Good old DaemonBurgers. Even I could afford to go here on rare occasions before.

"I've always admired the hustling skills of Peter Reiner," Lynn said. "*Iitadekimasu.*"

"Who?" I asked.

"The CEO of DaemonBurgers. They said it couldn't be done. They said he couldn't get enough magisters to be franchisees. They were wrong. Then they said he couldn't survive the new regime." She smiled. "They didn't know I was a fan. I sorted out the magister licensing rules so this can even exist."

"Good choice," I agreed. With Lynn's power, I realized, she could destroy entire industries like I might accidentally knock over a glass of milk.

As if reading my thoughts, Lynn continued, "People want me to ban all sorts of things. Why bother working to make a more competitive business when you can get a de facto Imperial monopoly? Oh, they don't put it that way. 'Think of all the jobs!' Yes, I do think about them. I know the monthly unemployment figures."

"Damned if you do, damned if you don't," I suggested.

"Basically." She looked around, then added in a whisper. "That applies to *everything* I do. But let's talk about something else."

"Let's," I agreed.

"Oh *crap* they found us!" Lynn said, getting up. I looked out the windows to see newsvans setting up. "Hurry!" She muttered and snapped her fingers and the bags started orbiting me. I hurried after her.

"Your Imperial Majesty!"

"Mr. Mason!"

"Could you comment on—!"

"Can you teleport us?" I asked.

"Me, yes, you, no. Run!"

Lynn was not merely practically flying, she was literally hovering over the ground. I was a fit guy. Together we outran them pretty easily.

A few minutes later, I stopped to catch my breath.

"We should be safe now," Lynn said.

I looked around. The Capital was a clean city, but this was a dirtier part. Empty and abandoned buildings lay around us, like a forgotten part of paradise. Strange. Wasn't real estate in the Capital insanely expensive? A dingy man chewed tobacco on the concrete steps of one building.

I looked at the bags orbiting me. "Do we really need all these?"

"Not really," she said. "Just insurance against poison."

"How about we give them out?"

She looked at me for a moment. "Sure."

We walked up to the man. "Hungry?" she asked.

He looked at the two of us. He spat out the tobacco. "What's the catch?"

"No catch," Lynn said. "*Ataenasai.*" A bag left my orbit and went to the guy.

He gripped it instantly. "Follow me." He motioned with his bag. We passed men, women, even a family with a child, and Lynn passed out bags. Too soon, we had run out.

I looked at Lynn. Couldn't she do something that would fix this? But she shook her head slightly, sadly.

Maybe she *could* do something. But she might have judged it would cause some worse evil. At least she tried to feed them, and didn't ship them back to Italy to make them someone else's problem.

Or maybe she *couldn't* do anything. The poor we will always have with us.

"I'll be back tomorrow," I promised them.

Lynn patted me on the shoulder. "Good idea."

Back at one of the Palace's studios, I was still thinking about what we had seen in those back alleys. Daemons put makeup on me, and another set were putting makeup on Lynn.

"Let's kiss," Lynn suggested. "Just so people know for certain."

"Sounds like a plan."

We went up in front of the cameras. I realized I wasn't afraid of them, which was great, because the paparazzi would be back. For the rest of my life, if everything went like I hoped.

"Three, two, one."

"Imperial citizens," Lynn began. "I'd like to quell rumors about my relationship with Mike here. We've had some ups and downs, but we are officially a couple now."

I thought it would be artificial to kiss on command, but as her lips met mine I didn't care if the world was watching. I felt nothing but her and her softness.

We broke off. "That is all," Lynn said.

"Good cut, I'd say," the director said. "I suggest we broadcast it as-is."

"I agree," I said.

"Sure," Lynn said. "How about some anime after this, Mike?"

My best day ever was only getting better as we shared a couch in front of the screen. Every now and then I would squeeze her hand.

When it was finished, though, I felt a little sadness. "I wish Mom was here. I want you to meet her."

"Maybe we can. I'm told that they should be released from the quarantine facility soon. No one's been hurt except for your fisherman friend, but he's adapting to the prosthesis pretty well."

"What about Kyle?" I asked.

"He's still in there."

"Why?" I asked.

She didn't quite meet my eyes. My stomach clenched in dread.

"Why, Lynn?"

She met my eyes and spoke calmly. "We've reviewed the transcripts of Ryan's contact and his subsequent conversations. There's no way around this: he's now a suspect in the overall investigation. He faces a charge of unlawful daemonology at best, terrorism or even treason at worst."

9

An Omelet of People

"Kyle? You can't be serious!" But the moment the words left my mouth I thought again. Kyle mouthed off all the time... Could he really have done something serious?

Lynn was unmoved. "In the initial transcript, he mentioned a mother daemon. That's a daemonology term of art for the daemon that binds the other daemons in the SMT. How would he know about it, if he was innocent?"

"But..." But what? I couldn't think of another explanation.

"We also examined his house in Lumberton and found buried pieces of improperly drawn diagrams, the sort new magisters make when they're learning daemonology."

Kyle, what did you do? "But he wouldn't have done all this," I protested.

"No, and he couldn't have had the capacity to even summon the mother daemon. But he might have assisted." Lynn paused. "Do you see how serious this is? The Old Magisterium would have a summary execution warrant for him at this point."

"You... you wouldn't do that."

"No. I stopped that. But I don't hand out pardons like candy."

I sighed.

"I would have pardoned him for your sake, but he is neither repentant or cooperative. Each day he has a completely new and more ridiculous claim. Recently he's been posing as a resistance movement leader."

Typical Kyle. But now he was in real trouble. "I might be able to talk to him."

Lynn raised an eyebrow. "Is he close?"

"My best friend."

"Then maybe you can knock some sense into him. And visit your family while you're at it."

"Let's do that," I said with relief. God, Kyle, why did you have to do this? I still believed he wouldn't go that far, but Lynn wouldn't joke about this.

Lynn had chosen an entirely different outfit for our trip—still all black, but with sturdier fabric. "It's out in the woods," she said.

I had worn my usual lumberjack clothing, a white T-shirt with denim over-alls. I figured if I looked normal, it would go over better that I was with the Witch-Queen.

Wherever we were going, it wasn't in the Capital.

We talked the whole way, then watched an anime called *Sekai no Iudex*. But I couldn't concentrate. All I could think of was my family, my friends, and Kyle.

"It" turned out to be a literal camp of colored dirty tents in the woods, sprawling over a clearing like an endless trash heap of people. Lynn looked out the window silently. "I'm not sure where we land."

"I don't think this place has aircar landing pads," I said.

"We'll land on the road, then." Lynn muttered orders, and with a bit of a thump, we landed.

I had expected the place to smell. It didn't, but it was if resignation and despair permeated the air. Lynn looked just about as affected by the atmosphere. "Keep an eye out," she ordered the servants, and walked in.

We passed by refugees in mismatched clothing, looking on us with fear and not a little anger and hate. A middle-aged women hanging clothes shooed her children into the tent at sight. Another set of children screamed "Witch-Queen!" and ran when they saw us.

Lynn looked around, her frozen expression hiding genuine distress.

"This whole place isn't Lumberton, is it?" I asked.

"No," she murmured. "I tried to limit the violence when I defeated the Old Magisterium. Not all my own forces listened." She paused. "And then there were people who would rather run than serve me."

If anyone here wanted to make a noble last stand by trying to punch her in the face, no one tried it. I could see Lynn muttering as she looked around, and I could swear I saw the air be a little hazy from moment to moment.

"Do you have any idea where our village is?"

"That is a good question. Let's head to the center."

The central buildings of the camp were sheer luxury: corrugated roof buildings and actual doors and windows. Two looked like communal showers, one was labeled "Mess Hall" and one building had a dirty Imperial flag hanging in front of it.

Inside, the worn man in charge of the refugee camp—whatever his official title was—looked more concerned than the Witch-Queen would cause a new headache for him than that he was talking to the Imperatrix Mundi.

"What do you want?" he snapped. "Your Imperial Majesty," he added as an afterthought.

"Where are the Lumberton displaced persons?" Lynn asked.

"In the west. Huge new clearing."

"Thank you," Lynn said.

The man returned to the binder he was reading.

We stepped outside. "Where's west?" I asked.

Lynn got out a tablet and looked. "That way," she said.

I couldn't help but look over her shoulder. I had never seen a real gravity mapper, and it didn't look like it did in the movies. The real thing was a lot smaller, thickly sturdy, and complicated with all sorts of buttons and knobs. But when she pinch-zoomed out, I saw how huge this place was.

It sprawled off in every direction. Were there thousands of people here? No, easily tens of thousands. How many eggs had Lynn cracked to make her omelet?

Lynn paused for a fraction of a second, then snapped her fingers. "We'll be walking for a bit."

I could tell Lynn was getting more and more disturbed the longer we were here. The names she chanted became softer, more halting. But what could I say? "This wasn't your fault"?

The ground was uneven and not even free of grass. I was used to hiking, so it was nothing to me, but I noticed Lynn was once again flying a little off the ground.

"Hey! You!" A man shouted, stepping in front of us. Others stopped to watch.

"Yes?" Lynn asked softly.

"We're going to kick your ass!" The man waved a tiny card in the air. "I'm still an American citizen, damn it!"

"And you're also an Imperial Citizen," Lynn said with a slight smile.

The man disagreed with this idea, offering numerous colorful suggestions on what she could do with Imperial citizenship.

"Hey, man," I interrupted.

"Traitor!"

"Dude, chill. What exactly are you going to do here?"

He glared, hatred and anger transferred from Lynn to me.

"If you want to protest your treatment, here she is. But can you even hurt her? No."

"The USA will rise again!"

"Dave, stop harassing her!" A woman dragged him off. "She can level this whole place, you know."

"We have to manure the tree of liberty with her blood!" the man protested.

Lynn looked even more distressed.

"Let's keep moving," I suggested.

We kept moving.

The Lumberton section was relatively new. "Mike!" a little girl squealed, running up to me.

"Hello, Emily," I said, patting her pigtails.

"Are you the Witch-Queen?" she asked Lynn.

"I am," Lynn said, with the second smile I had seen on her in this place.

"They say all sorts of mean things about you here," Emily confided.

"That's unfortunate," Lynn agreed.

"I'll tell everyone you're here." She sped off, shouting "Mike's back!"

"I guess we're here." I walked further in. I recognized a lot of people here, and conversely, everyone recognized me.

Some of the looks were no longer friendly.

Damn it, what could I do? I wouldn't give up on Lynn just because my friends were angry at their situation. Even if—

I saw Mom hurry to us. *Mike!* she signed.

Mom! I signed back, hurried to her and hugged her in a bear hug. *This is Lynn.*

Hello, Lynn, Mom signed.

"My mom is deaf," I explained, but Lynn snapped and a typewriter appeared in the air.

"Here, Mrs. Mason," Lynn said, and the typewriter typed that out. She handed it to Mom.

"Thank you," she typed.

A crowd gathered around us.

Come on, let's go inside, Mom signed.

Sure thing, I signed back. "Come on," I told Lynn.

She stopped outside the tent door.

"What?" I asked.

"Checking for traps," she said. "It's not you! Anywhere can be dangerous."

Don't worry about it, Mom signed. The calm on her face was communication enough for Lynn.

Inside, the tent was neat, but it was still a tent. A laundry basket, a folding table with a camp chair, and a sleeping bag were its only contents. "Lynn, what about all our stuff?"

She snapped her fingers and more folding chairs appeared. "We systematically examined and cataloged every object in your village," Lynn said. "Which is one reason we had to evacuate everyone. You can bind a daemon to nearly any object. But it's all safe in a warehouse right now."

Mom typed. "There should be a fragment of a bottle cap in a frame."

"Like I said, a warehouse. I can get it for you if you want, but believe me, there was no looting, no throwing away, no leaving for the elements. The SMP Suspicious Object Division are professionals."

"Thank you."

For the third time, Lynn smiled a little.

How are you doing, Mom? I signed.

It's been stressful, but things are OK. We just got here yesterday. Still learning the ins and outs of this place.

I translated for Lynn.

"I'm sorry you had to go through this," she said.

"I understand, Lynn," Mom typed. "They showed us what happened to Marty Mac. He's doing fine, too, by the way. He decided to get a hook instead of a prosthetic hand. Says he likes the idea better."

"You're safe here," I reassured her.

"How are you?" Mom typed for Lynn. "I haven't talked to Mike in a while, and we've just met."

"Things are going great," I said. "We're officially a couple now—you probably saw." Lynn kissed me on the cheek and I blushed.

"I can't talk about details, but things are going good for me, too." Lynn snapped her fingers, and a ream of paper popped out, as well as a box of ink ribbons. "For you."

"You don't need to go to all this trouble," Mom replied.

"I know. You've got it all managed already, I'm sure. But if you need to go somewhere where people don't know ASL, now you're all set."

"I don't want to go anywhere. I want to go back to Lumberton."

Lynn pressed a lever on the typewriter, which stopped typing. "Mike, can you translate for me? I don't want a print record of this floating around."

"Sure," I said.

"Mrs. Mason, we are faced with what's called a Summoning Minus Termination scenario. Someone bound a daemon that binds other daemons without limit. Until we track down the mother daemon, it's not safe."

Didn't you destroy it already? Mom asked.

"We unbound *one,* but as long as the mother daemon's on the loose, there's an unlimited number of them out there. We're still investigating, and we haven't found a culprit."

I think Mom could tell I knew Lynn wasn't being fully truthful, but she didn't call us on it. *Will you ever find it?*

"Every counter-revolutionary slips up eventually. Every last one."

Someone knocked on a doorpost. *It's Grandpa Franklin!* I signed, and went out the flap to let him in.

"Mike!" he said, and hugged me. "And Your Imperial Majesty." He fell silent, and made a very small genuflection.

Lynn pressed the typewriter again. "At ease," she said softly.

"I have to admit, I never thought I'd see you in person," Grandpa Franklin said, looking her over.

"I hear that a lot," Lynn said.

"I'd normally offer you a soda, but this is Belinda's house, and there's nothing here but MREs."

Lynn paused for the slightest moment. "I understand."

"If you'd allow us to hunt, we'd be much better off."

"With depleted wildlife and more weapons floating around?"

Grandpa Franklin nodded. "So you have thought about it."

"In general, yes. I haven't investigated every single situation in the Empire."

"Then let me ask you a question, ma'am: why did you do this?"

"We're still searching for the rogue daemons that tainted the water supply," Lynn said. Interesting, that she told a slightly different story to him.

"That's what they've told us. But that's not what I meant. Why did you make yourself World Empress?"

"To make the world a better place," Lynn replied without hesitation.

Grandpa Franklin stretched out his hands. "And this is better?"

"There are no more wars. 99% of the world now has food security. Every dominion has religious freedom. No dominion is denied daemonology. I dare say the world has improved."

"But what about *here*?"

Lynn fell silent for a moment.

I'll ask her eventually, Grandpa Franklin signed back to Mom.

I turned to Mom. *What?*

Lynn looked puzzled.

I was asking about Kyle, Mom signed.

"We're talking about Kyle," I told Lynn. "This is his grandfather."

"He isn't a bad boy," Grandpa said.

"No. But he's become a suspect in the investigation," Lynn said.

"Why?"

"I can't comment on investigations."

"I won't tell anyone," Grandpa Franklin persisted.

Lynn sighed. "We found evidence he was involved in high-level daemonology."

"High-level?" I asked.

"The diagrams he was building parts of were for something above a Rank V. Which is, conveniently, what we're looking for."

"Kyle wouldn't have done this!" Grandpa almost shouted.

"He wouldn't have done this if he knew the consequences. But the first rule of daemonology is this: know the consequences of your actions. A good rule for life, too."

"Then look around you, Witch-Queen!" Grandpa Franklin yelled, as angry as his grandson. "These are the consequences of *your* actions!"

"I know," Lynn said calmly.

Mom typed away rapidly, then pulled out the page and handed it to Lynn. "Lynn, I don't agree with all of your actions, but you've at least tried to make the world a better place. Even if you don't always succeed."

"Is there something I can do to make this part of the world better?" Lynn asked.

Mom typed. "Why not ask everyone else? We just got here."

Lynn got up. For one moment, I saw her shoulders slightly slump in weariness. "I will."

There was a massive crowd outside. When Lynn and I emerged, there were boos and hisses, even from people I knew. I wanted to shout that she wasn't that bad, but how could I say that with a straight face *here*?

"Tell the rest of the camp," Lynn called out. "I'm making a speech in the center."

News traveled at the speed of light. By the time we arrived in the center the crowd had already gathered.

Not everyone, though. Some were probably afraid she would kill them all, I realized. But *I* knew Lynn wouldn't do that.

Lynn stood on a stage she had materialized. She spoke in Japanese briefly, and then her voice was really, *really* loud. "I am Lynn. Yes, the real Witch-Queen. I see life isn't so great here, and that's at least partially my fault. So how about I help you out? What do you need most?"

"Yeah, right!" a teenager shouted. "You're just trying to bribe us!"

Murmurs and booing broke out.

"You can't have it both ways," Lynn said. "Either I am ruining your life, or trying to bribe you. Pick one."

A old man shouted something obscene, waving his card. A Social Security card, now that I saw it. "Give us money!"

"I can do that."

"But not in the bank! Real money."

"That's a bit more difficult."

"I want to live a normal life without kneeling to your goddamn royal ass!" a woman screamed.

"You're an Imperial Citizen. Nothing changes if you get the ID card."

"Like hell it does! You just want everything for yourself, you power-hungry bitch!"

"Hey, shut up," a man shouted to her. "Your Imperial Majesty, we could really use running water."

"No! I want my retirement!" the old man yelled again.

"Screw retirements!" a teenager piped up. "You want to make us happy? Leave us alone!"

"How about you bring back the dead, Ms. *Witch*-Queen? Not omnipotent, are you?"

"No, I'm not omnipotent," Lynn said. "So pick *one* thing. Do you want me to resettle you all in a town?"

"Screw that! America will rise again!"

"Please, Your Imperial Majesty, we want more food! It's terrible here."

"Hey, can I get your autograph?" a teenage girl asked.

"Just *stop* already!" Lynn shouted. With her amplified voice, it was deafening. "Yes, this is a awful situation. I can't fix all of your lives at once."

"You ruined all of them at once!" a girl shouted. Boos and hissing followed.

I could tell Lynn was on the verge of tears. I didn't know what to do, then I did. I walked up to her and told her. "Lynn, give me the mic."

"*Maiku mo.*"

"Hey, everyone." My voice echoed off the trees. "Look at me. Listen to my accent. I'm from here. I'm not some random noble. I don't even have a title other than Companion to the Crown, and I'm pretty sure that doesn't count."

The crowd fell silent, watching me with suspicious eyes.

"Yes, this is a crappy situation. But Lynn here is offering to make one thing—*one* thing better. No, she can't bring back the dead. No, she's not going to undo the Empire. But for your own sakes, surely there's something you want that will ease your suffering? Why make a stupid stand when your welfare is at stake?"

"Traitor! That's what she said!"

"And she was right. Remember how things badly sucked during the War? Hyperinflation, food shortages, constant violence? Whatever you think of her now, things are better. Hell, at least you all have MREs to eat."

The crowd murmured and shifted.

"How about a well?" I asked. "Running water for all of you?"

"How about a well for *all* refugee camps?" a woman demanded. "We're not the only ones."

"I'll build wells everywhere," Lynn promised. "As much water as anyone needs. Everywhere in the world."

The crowd didn't react.

"Anyone got another idea?" I asked.

"Toilet paper!" a man shouted.

"We already have enough of it, you idiot!" a guy next to him said.

"Not for me!"

The crowd fell into bickering. "Wells it is," Lynn said. "Expect it in a month or two. And I'll see if I can get you all more toilet paper."

The crowd laughed, nervous but disarmed.

"Dismissed."

We walked back to the limo, remarkably undisturbed. "I need...to be somewhere quiet," Lynn said.

"The forest is. Follow me."

"There's no roads there!"

"We don't need any," I told her. "It's just the outdoors."

Lynn sighed, but followed me into the trees.

Pretty soon, she was looking around with wonder. "What a strange place."

"Really?"

"I've never actually been in the wilderness before. I think the one time I went camping was with Vasyl and—some friends," she said. "Lost ones."

"I'm sorry."

"Not your fault. Ow!" She bounced back from the root she had almost tripped over.

"Oh, yeah, watch your step."

"I will."

We walked through the forest in silence.

"Do you know where we are?" she asked.

"Don't worry about it. You can teleport and have the mapper. I know how to survive. We'll be fine."

She sighed. "When you have power, it's fun at first. Then everyone comes out of the woodwork, demanding you fix their crap. A good number are reasonable. And then there are the people who get upset about taxes, or healthcare, or the metric system, or that they got out of the wrong side of bed that morning, or every morning, or that oranges are round, or heavens knows what. All of them come to *me*."

"And you can't do everything."

"I can't. One time, I had a petitioner whose petition was that the plumbing in his government housing was broken. I know how serious that can be, and he said it was an ongoing problem. So I had my thirty-second audience with him." She sighed again. "The water was hot in the summer and cold in the winter."

"That was his problem?"

"That was his problem. He spent his once-in-a-lifetime petition on complaining about the laws of thermodynamics. I told him I would consider it. And I did. I seriously thought about binding a thermodynamics daemon to regulate the temperature. But then *everyone* would want it. Next thing up, everyone wants oranges to be genetically engineered to be cubes."

I walked with her as she groaned.

"All of their complaints—well, most of them—could be fixed if I threw money at the problem. The problem is, nearly everyone here has no Imperial

ID, or they wouldn't be here to begin with. I'm constantly building more government housing."

"Why not just give them cash?"

"I can't. I made promises, Mike. Promises that you'd get a certain exchange rate, or certain bonuses, or, heck, outright privileges. I can't give those to people who didn't take me on my *limited-time* offer. I can't go back on my word and let the world fall into chaos." Lynn sighed once more. "And no, I can't just release the restrictions on Imperial IDs, even if they are citizens by law. The entire world's economic infrastructure is based around Imperial IDs. Taxation alone—ah!"

I had grabbed her elbow to pull her back before she stepped on the snake.

"What the—AAIEEEGH!!!" Lynn literally flew into the air.

"That's just a Florida Scarletsnake," I reassured her. "Look: 'Red on black, a friend of Jack.'"

"I'd prefer my interactions with ophidians not be moderated by *any* nursery rhyme, thanks," Lynn replied, still hovering.

"It probably wouldn't have even bit you."

"Let's go somewhere else. We still haven't visited Kyle."

If Lynn had been disturbed by the refugee camp, she was far more unsettled by the prison we landed in. There was no opening to the sky, only a solid concrete shell encasing the complex. And it *was* a complex. When they let us through the gate, numerous sub-buildings were spread across the dead earth inside.

Lynn's eyes were glued to one, but the guards—all magisters—led to another larger building. We left the fake, fluorine-lit sky that was insultingly painted blue, and Lynn seemed slightly less on edge.

Most of the cells were empty. "We've had a recent lull in cases," an SMP agent cheerfully told us. "Everything is shipshape!"

Which probably meant things were a total hellhole here, I thought, but Lynn didn't react. We turned a corner and—

"Kyle? Are you OK, man?"

He had been thin last I saw him, and now he was almost skeletal. A hunger strike? Poor nutrition? Stress? He looked at us with exhausted, fearful eyes, which widened as soon as he recognized me. "Get away from him!" he shouted.

"Kyle, chill, she's my girlfriend."

"She tricked you! She doesn't really care for you!"

"Shut up!" I said. "Do you have any idea how much trouble you're in?"

"It's... It's all worth it for the cause," he sniffled.

"You talk," Lynn told me. "*Teikoku no onsha o kudasai.*" She snapped her fingers, and a clipboard with a fancy form appeared in her hands.

"Listen to me, man," I said to Kyle. "Do you know what the daemon you helped summon did?"

"There was no daemon!"

"Like hell there wasn't! What the hell did they find in your room?"

"It wasn't in my..." Kyle shut up.

"Did they show you what happened to Marty Mac?"

Kyle looked away.

"Answer me, Kyle. Do you know the consequences of your actions?"

"You... can't break an omelet..."

"For God's sake, Kyle, *Marty Mac*! We're all homeless because of you."

Kyle didn't reply.

Lynn showed him the form. "This is an Imperial Pardon."

"No!" Kyle screamed.

"Shut your trap," I said. "Kyle, do you realize how serious this is? Maybe you're still deluded, but for once in your entire life look around you and stop pretending to be a revolutionary! You're facing a charge of treason! That means death, you idiot!"

Kyle stopped.

"Your grandpa asked about you. What am I going to tell him? That you were too much of an idiot to take the way out when you could?"

"No," he whimpered.

"This is an Imperial Pardon," Lynn repeated. "But you'll note that it doesn't have the Imperial Seal on it. You see, I don't give pardon to the unrepentant."

"I will never repent!"

"Kyle," I warned. "Everything that happened to our village is at least partially your fault. Legal consequences aside, do you think this was pleasing to God? Do you want this on your conscience?

Kyle was Protestant, but my logic got through. "I'll... repent. I'm... I'm sorry," he said. Then started crying.

"First," Lynn said. "Tell us the real story. Not all three hundred lies. The real story."

"I... I was in an online group. One of those retro MMORPGs. Met some people." He wiped his eyes. "I didn't mean anything wrong. We just joked about things. About... your Empire." He looked at Lynn as if he had never imagined she was a real human being. "Some of them weren't jokes. A guy DM'd me and said he knew a friend who was into action, if I knew what he meant."

Neither Lynn or I spoke.

"I met him. There were about twenty of us in the room. He said—I don't remember what he looked like, I swear to God, he spoke from behind a curtain. He gave us this PowerPoint presentation on what he wanted made. I was a carpenter, so he gave me instructions on how to make diagrams. It's... it's harder than it looks."

"It is," Lynn agreed. "Did you have more contact with him?"

"No. He said to leave the completed—he wanted these wooden boards—to be left at a certain location."

I could tell by the slightest shift in her expression that Lynn was suddenly alarmed, and not just freaking out about the prison. "Can you mark on a map where they told you to leave it?"

"Yes. I memorized the coordinates."

"I'll let you talk to the professionals, then." Lynn snapped her fingers and a ink pad and a large circular seal appeared in the air. She stamped it on the Pardon. "After that, you're free to go."

Kyle had the constipated expression of a man who is trying not to let words leak out, but they broke through anyway. "Thank you."

"Let him out!" she called to the guards.

Kyle hugged me with a weak grasp and genuflected to her.

"Why were you so upset?" I asked, on the ride back home. Lynn had said that the SMP would take Kyle back to the camp with the rest of Lumberton.

"I don't like prisons. They freak me out."

"No, I mean about the diagram."

Lynn said a few more names, then met my eyes. "Most summoning diagrams are compact, because the higher the rank, the bigger they can get. We usually track down high-level daemonology by the diagrams, since they're almost always outdoors. Most magisters don't even know you can make a diagram spread out over a distance in several parts."

"But you can, apparently."

"Yes. So far we've thought this is a rogue American magister, from when the US tried to reinvent not merely the wheel, but the entire car, as my forces took control. There is no way they figured out how to make a partitioned diagram. I spent months trying to figure it out on the Moon with no success. So some high-level survivor of the Old Magisterium is out there."

"Wanting it to come back."

"Well, that, too. From what we've seen, though, they want revenge."

10

THE MASON FOUNDATION

I thought about it. Five years ago, I would have celebrated someone standing up to the Witch-Queen, but now... What had I come to? Several hours ago I had been an apologist for the Empire.

"Something wrong?" Lynn asked.

"Just how life changes," I said.

"It does. Let's do something else," Lynn said. "More *Sekai no Iudex?*"

"Sure," I said. Anything else.

Two hours later we had finished the whole season. I savored the theme song, *Reaction MASS*, because it was a banger, and even if the show *had* ended on a cliffhanger....

"When we get back I'll get the next season," Lynn said.

"There was no second season."

"What?"

"Look at the copyright date: 2030. Just when daemons were discovered and science fiction and fantasy stopped being so fun."

Lynn frowned. "And they *had* to end it on a cliffhanger."

I shrugged. "That's what they did in that era. Make 13 episodes and then hope they got renewed. And then stopped renewing any."

"Hmm." Lynn looked distant. "Let's... I don't know."

"I'm just sleepy. How long until we're home?"

"Another six hours, I think."

"I need to rest."

"So do I." Lynn snapped her fingers and a bed appeared. "Uh..."

Now what? I had been told to avoid sleeping in the same bed with a girl before marriage, even chastely. But there were two of us and one bed. Not that I would *mind,* but I—Oh, wait, if we shared a bed I'd be incinerated from touching her. "Lynn, if you wouldn't mind going home—"

Lynn had evidentially been making the same calculation. "I'm not leaving. I need to be here in case someone tries to shoot this aircar down."

"What are the chances of that?" I asked.

"Too high to risk it. You take the bed, I'll put up a divider and sleep on the couch."

"All right. But I'd like to sleep on the couch."

"I've slept on nearly *everything,*" Lynn insisted. "I had to, when I was a revolutionary."

"I've slept on uneven ground outside without a sleeping bag," I counter-insisted.

"Fine. You win." Lynn got up, snapped her fingers again, and a curtain appeared. "*Oyasumi.*"

"*Oyasumi,*" I replied, the traditional Japanese "Good night."

I crawled across the couch, feeling the warmth where she had sat. Yeah, I wasn't going to sleep tonight.

On the other hand, I had jet lag on my side. I closed my eyes and—

Lynn screamed. I snapped awake and tore down the curtain to see her thrashing in her bed. "Lynn!" I called, and grabbed her.

She shoved me away with superhuman force. *"Namae no hon o kudasai!"* she shouted, and a thick tome appeared. She frantically paged through it, like a man losing his faith would search the Bible for any kind of answer. At last she sighed, snapped her fingers, and the book disappeared.

"Nightmare?" I asked, kneeling by her side.

"I have PTSD. Really, *really* bad PTSD." She looked around. "What time is it?"

I checked my cellphone. 7 AM Imperial Time. According to the GPS, we were close to the Capital. "We're almost home."

"Great." She breathed deeply. "I... need to be alone for a bit."

I put the curtain back up.

Lynn kissed me goodbye outside of my apartment. "See ya!" She snapped her fingers and disappeared.

The first thing I wanted do was go back to sleep. I walked inside to find Alice waiting for me with a pile of magazines on the coffee table.

"What the hell are you doing here?" I asked.

"Just here with some advice," she said.

"I really need to... sleep..." I trailed off when I saw the top magazine. *Weddings Tomorrow.* "For God's sake, Alice—"

"For *humanity's* sake," she interrupted. "Lynn's happy and stable right now. She'd be even more stable if you started sleeping with each other—"

"Listen, we were in separate beds..." I facepalmed at my own words. "I didn't say that."

"Ah, so you're already on the way," Alice said with a smile.

"Alice, we've been officially a couple for a few *days.*"

"Then give it a few more weeks. Considering the sort of trashy romance novels the Imperatrix reads—"

I groaned. "Just..."

She pulled out a jewelry magazine from the stack. "Don't worry about the cost. I'll bankroll you. For all of our sakes."

"Right now, the roll I want is a *bed* roll. By myself."

"But the sooner you marry, the sooner you can share it."

"Alice!"

"Well?" She continued to smile.

I sighed deliberately. "Yes, I'm attracted to her. But I have standards. I'm going to treat her like a decent human—"

"Then marry her. My husband proposed to me in the first week."

"Please, Alice, I've been on a long trip, and I didn't get much sleep—"

"Oh?" she raised an eyebrow.

"For God's sake, it was just because she woke up screaming."

Alice instantly turned serious.

"She... she said she has PTSD," I explained.

"She never said anything about that to me, though I'm not surprised."

"She had this book and frantically looked through it. I have no idea what that was about."

"I know she has a book with the list of all her daemons. Most high magisters have something like that. But I wouldn't know, either." She looked at me in the eyes. "You are the one human being alive who she really trusts. You can save us all. And that starts—"

"With me getting some sleep," I finished. "Give me time, all right?"

"As long as you realize how much destruction Lynn can cause when she's angry." Alice muttered in Latin and disappeared.

I looked at the magazines. For all my arguing, truth was, part of me *did* want to have her right away, in every sense of the term.

Amanda and I had talked about it. But considering how *that* ended, I didn't want to repeat the experience. No, I needed to make sure, first. Make sure that this was what I wanted, and I was ready, and so was Lynn.

I got out my rosary. Time to keep her in my prayers.

Kyle was on trial for treason, in a kangaroo court in a corrugated-roof building, and I kept arguing for his innocence, but every time I said something the SMP would present some new evidence, and Kyle would say something stupider, and Lynn sat there on the judge's bench and watched...

I woke up, relieved it was only a nightmare.

I staggered out into my apartment, but then realized what I hadn't noticed due to both Alice and jet lag: it was different. What were all those boxes?

One had a note.

> Hey, Mike, I realized you could use your stuff. So here it is! I even got that framed bottle cap that your mom talked about. xoxoxo Lynn, I.M.

I opened up the box to see the soft green form of Ellie the Elephant inside a clear evidence bag.

I first felt disconcerted, then violated, then relieved. I pulled her out and stroked her felt. I had been super attached to my stuffed animals for a long time. Still was, I realized. Nostalgia flooded through me. Ellie looked back with her unchanged eager eyes, as if wondering what adventures her master had gone on to without her.

I put Ellie back in the box. I would need to put her somewhere safe, as well as the rest of my old friends. And speaking of putting things away, I would have to hide the wedding magazines, lest Lynn see them.

Please God, I prayed, *Let Lynn not have arrived when I was asleep and seen all of them.*

I found a cabinet to stick the magazines in, and... another cabinet to stick the box of my stuffed animals in, *after* I had removed them from the evidence bags. The rest of the boxes could wait.

I walked out to the mail room and checked my mail. The mailbox was crammed full of letters.

I squeezed it out and sorted through it. Most was junk, and most of that was charities asking for my money. Then there was a thick envelope from Monte Carlo Casino. "Time to face the music," I grumbled to myself as I opened it.

Dear Mr. Michael Mason

We sincerely apologize for your treatment—

What the hell? I had been out of line and they apologized to *me?*

I scanned down the page of increasing amounts of literary chest-beating and then tore the letter in two. The rest of the envelope was various logistical details about my winnings, including a check. I had won a little under 2 million IM, from the money I already won or gotten from Lynn.

Yeah, I still needed to apologize to the asshole, and what would I do with the money?

The thought now disgusted me. Look at me, in a practical palace in *the* Palace, and my friends and family lived in tents... How could I even...

Wait a minute.

A thought entered my mind.

I got out my cellphone and dialed Alice.

"Yes?" she asked eagerly.

"Could you come over here? I want to talk to you."

She popped into my vision in a literal instant. "What do you need?"

"Uh, this isn't about *that.* "

She looked at me with a raised eyebrow.

"Just give me time," I pleaded. "Listen, I..." The idea sounded crazy. "I want to start a charity."

"Certainly. What do you want?"

"I want to create a fund to resettle people in refugee camps."

"How are you planning to do this? Have you researched why they're there?"

"Lynn said that they needed money," I said. I held up the check. "I have money."

"I'm not sure what you're planning, but that's not enough. Are you thinking of unconditional cash payments, building new housing...?"

"New housing."

"Two million will buy you four to nine houses, or one apartment building in a poor area."

I frowned.

"I'm not discouraging you," Alice said. "I have this conversation with the Imperatrix regularly, whenever she wants to give more money away. Money doesn't always go as far as it sounds."

"What does she do?"

"She issues an Imperial Grant. Which I'm sure she'll do for you." Alice winked. "You can also get Royal Grants from local dominions."

"All right," I said. "How do I set it up?"

"It may take a bit, but we can move fast. I would recommend starting as soon as possible, to avoid Lynn's mood shifting and her getting bored."

"Right," I said. "Let's get started."

A large amount of money has an amazing ability: it puts life on fast-forward. Two weeks later, the Mason Foundation had an office in the Capital and a meeting set up with a huge number of donors.

His Royal Highness Prince Frederik of the Scandinavian dominion was among them.

I decided not to have a fit about it. In any case, my life was going just fine. Lynn was frequently busy, but she fit in time with me whenever she could. I didn't broach the subject of the Big M, nor did she, but I wondered if she was thinking about it already, too.

But whatever. I showed up that Friday in a fancy suit to see the donors had already gathered. Most of Lynn's friends were already there, talking and joking with each other. I recognized a few celebrities, as well as a tall, dark-skinned man who everyone seemed to look at with envy.

"The man of the hour!" Raphael toasted me with a glass of some white liquid. "And the genius behind it all."

Genius? The only thing I had done was actually care about the plight of refugees. Alice and some staff she had hired had done basically all the work. "You are too kind," I said, and took a seat.

My CEO, Walter Johnson, a bald, accountant-looking man, opened up a suitcase and passed out brochures. "We're looking for approximately 120 million IM for the first resettlement site," he said. "It depends where we build it, but to give access to jobs, it needs to be near a relatively wealthy area."

"120 million?" Raphael asked. "I can contribute ten million right off the bat."

"I will have to rearrange my finances, but I can also contribute a substantial sum," Albert said. "It really depends *where* the site is located."

"I don't suppose we've been introduced," the tall man said, and stretched out a hand. "Peter Reiner."

Oh, yeah, the CEO of DaemonBurgers. He was probably the wealthiest guy in the room. "Michael Mason," I said.

"I'm usually interested in rebuilding projects," he said. "Which is why I'm wondering why we aren't simply rebuilding areas that were destroyed."

"We've considered that, but without use of eminent domain, we cannot guarantee that the present owners of devastated land will sell to us," Johnson interjected. "It will be more cost-effective to buy empty land."

"I'm concerned about environmental effects," Chen said.

"Pah, we could fit the whole Empire into my subdominion," Raphael said.

"Not without cutting down most of the trees inside!"

"I'm certain we can arrange more eco-friendly constructions," Albert said.

"Yes, we're currently doing a study on that, but my estimate is for another one hundred million IM," Johnson said.

As the numbers grew bigger and bigger without any reaction from the other donors, I felt smaller and smaller. These people could have done this all without even feeling a pinch. The fact that *I* was doing it made all the difference.

I looked around. They *looked* sincere. Maybe they were. But what was ten million IM to buy influence with Lynn? Peter Reiner gave me a curious look. I gave one back.

Frederik met my eyes. I couldn't read him, but I knew whatever he was here for...

"If I may interrupt," he interrupted. "While it's good and all to know where the displaced persons are going to, where are they coming *from?* After all, Mr. Mason's family and friends are currently in a camp."

I wasn't going to fall for it. "As we've all seen in the brochure, we're going to resettle refugees based on how long they've been in the camps. It's the only fair way."

"But why not jump ahead for your family?" Raphael asked with sincere curiosity.

"You could arrange it easily with a lottery," Albert mused. "No one will know if we alter the results."

"I'm not corrupt," I said.

They all laughed.

All except Peter Reiner. "If we're going to engage in nepotism, I'm out. I have better things to do than to scratch the backs of the wealthy."

"We're not going to do that," I said. "We're going to make this fair."

"What's fair?" Lynn asked, walking inside. Everyone but me got up and bowed. "At ease."

"We're asking about whether family ties are more important than strict fairness," Frederik asked.

"I don't want to give my family special treatment, or I'm no better than—" I cut myself off. What, a royal?

"Then what do you want, Mike?" Lynn asked.

"I'm not sure what you mean," I said, heat rising in me.

"Do you want to help your village? The largest number of people? The people who have suffered the most? The people who are the most in need?"

"Most in need, I guess."

"Then you should pick based on the condition of the refugees."

"I would caution against a means-tested program," Peter Reiner said. "They have a habit of backfiring and keeping the poor in poverty."

"It'll be means-tested until they get the money," Albert said. "Then they're on their own, sink or swim. That's how I would arrange it."

"I agree," I said. "We should just give them some help, not take over their lives."

"Oh, I agree as well," Frederik said.

What was he planning?

"Of course, we of the Scandinavian Dominion have very harsh winters, and without public assistance our poor would literally die. Our systems are more set up for mass housing programs, so I would recommend we consider building the new settlements in our lands."

"No," I said, my voice raising. "Hell, no."

"Why not?" Frederik asked.

"What on Earth, Mike?" Lynn asked. "His proposal makes sense."

"If we're concerned about a certain incident," Frederik said. "let it be known that I have forgiven you fully."

"An incident?" Lynn asked.

"I'll tell you later," I said. "I'm... I'm sorry about it."

Frederik waved it away. "Water under the bridge."

"Look, it makes perfect sense to me," Raphael said. "I know the Duke of San Francisco's welfare policies keep failing."

"I think that's because it's so *nice* down there," Chen said dreamily. "If I was homeless, I would want to live there, too."

"Then perhaps we *should* build the settlement in the colder regions," Albert said. "It must be terrible to live in a tent in the winter."

"I'll have to look into the figures," Johnson said. "We'd have to spent more on heating."

No, no, no. This was all going wrong. I felt helpless in my own meeting. "Listen, why not build them in the North American dominions?" I asked. "They need jobs, too—"

"If they have jobs, they can live wherever they feel like," Chen said.

"Yeah, we're supposed to help, not make the gravy train for those who won't get off their asses," Raphael said.

"You know what they say," Frederik said. "Beggars can't be choosers."

I slammed the table with my fists, making it shudder so hard Raphael's drink spilled. "*Who the hell are you to lecture us*?!" I screamed. "All of you, living fat and healthy while the people starve. You call us lazy, when you haven't worked a goddamned day in your *goddamned lives*!"

They stared at me.

I stomped out into the hallway, the hallway of an office I owned, and slammed my fist against the wall, and again, and again. I was so angry I didn't even feel the pain.

What I had done?

I had to go back and apologize—

No. Screw them. I would rather us not have money than apologize to those rich bastards—

"Mike," Lynn said calmly from behind me.

"What is wrong with people?" I asked.

"Michael Mason. Turn and look at me."

I did. She looked at me with an unyielding frown, and despite our relative sizes I thought I was looking up at her presence.

"Look into my eyes, Mike."

I met her full-bore stare.

"If you want to change the world, you have to start by not alienating people. Even if you disagree with them. Even if you hate them."

"But..." I trailed off at the full intensity of her eyes.

"You barely know any of my friends. Some were nobles before I ruled. Some were just rich. Some were just ordinary citizens at the right time and place.

Peter Reiner grew up homeless. So before you shoot your mouth off again, and alienate people *who are trying to do what you asked,* THINK!"

"I'm... when... when we were growing up, we had no money," I said. "My dad... spent it all. And we were poor to begin with." And then we had lost most of our savings in the War, I didn't add.

"So what are you going to do?" Lynn asked, unmoved. "Live like a poor man in your brain for the rest of your life?"

"Better be poor than rot rich in Hell!" I shouted.

"Oh, really?" Lynn raised an eyebrow. "So you know who's going to Hell now?"

I shut up.

"Newsflash, Mike, the moment you became my Companion, you were set for life. You don't have to keep the money. You can give it away. You can spend it on wild parties. You can hate yourself for being rich. But what you *can't* do is judge other people who made different choices than you."

I took a deep breath. "But they had the choice to do whatever they wanted with their money, and we didn't."

"So? Some nations had more money, people, and resources than others. I decided to make things fair by equalizing all of that. And look how that turned out."

I blinked. That was the first time I had ever heard Lynn criticize one of her own decisions, especially one as major as the Redistricting.

"Do you get my point, Mike? This is how the world works. Either you accept that some people have more money and some people don't, and yes, it's often unfair, or you spend the rest of your life wallowing in jealousy and envy. No one in that room was responsible for you and your family being poor. If you want them to help of their own free will, you have to treat them with respect. *Look* at me, Mike."

I sighed and met her eyes again. I thought about arguing more, but I knew I had lost. "I'm sorry."

"Don't apologize to me. Apologize to *them.* "

"All right."

We walked back in together. The room had become icier since I left, and looks passed between the various individuals.

"I—I apologize for my remarks," I said. "I was out of line."

"Come," Peter Reiner said. "We've all had outbursts from time to time. No reason to dwell on them."

The room nodded along. Did they forgive me because I was with Lynn? Or were they sincere?

No, I told myself. I had no right to judge their forgiveness. Not if I wanted to treat them with respect.

"Let's just split the difference," Raphael said. "We build one site in the Scandinavian Dominion, and one in, I don't know, NAWD?"

"NAWD is *cold*," Chen said.

"Yes, all the more reason to build one there."

No, what had I been saying? They had a point. "If we have different camps, though, who goes where?"

"A lottery," Albert suggested. "We'd keep families together, obviously, but why should we make judgments ourselves? Or we could weight the lottery, based on income—"

"Damn it, Albert, why do you have to make everything so complicated?" Raphael said. "Just have a lottery and be done with it."

"Sounds like a plan, to me," Lynn said. "I can use the Imperial Bureau of Randomness for it."

"Yeah," I said. It would definitely be incorruptible, if Lynn picked the numbers. Probably. I wouldn't put it past Lynn to interfere, but I had a feeling she wanted *this*, at least, to be fair. "But what if we split up a community?"

"I don't see how we *couldn't*," Albert said. "There will always be more refugees than housing."

"At least for now," Frederik mused. "Once we build enough, we'll empty out the camps except for those who refuse to get Imperial IDs. And then they can live wherever they like."

"I'm willing to hand out benefits to those without IDs," Lynn said. "But only to move them to a place with heat and electricity. If they want jobs, they need to get an ID like anyone else. We can have up to twenty-five ID sites, so we can move them temporarily."

"Only twenty-five?" I asked.

"Only twenty-five." She did not explain further.

That was curious. Maybe there was something daemonic going on. But I wouldn't press Lynn about it. "So, two settlements to start with. We pick people—I mean, families—by a lottery. How much will that cost?"

John was calculating away on a smartphone. "Around five hundred million IM, I believe, if we're building in colder areas, but—"

"Oh, *snap,* got to go." Lynn disappeared.

Great. Now I was alone with *them.*

"Actually," Peter Reiner said immediately. "We need more hard figures, more donors at this point, and cooler heads. Let's just take a break."

"Yes," I said, relieved. I'd never imagined I'd be thankful for one of the richest men in the world saving my rear end, but I wasn't going to turn it down.

"Well, I'm off to drink," Raphael said. "Any care to join me?"

A few of them—us?—did. They all left, until it was just Frederik, Peter, and me.

"My apologies if anything I said offended you," Frederik said.

That was... bizarre, from him. "My apologies for the 'incident.'"

"Then let's leave it all in the past, I dare say." He nodded to me and walked out.

"Mr. Mason, a word," Peter Reiner said.

"Yes?" I asked.

"The rest are only in it for Her Imperial Majesty's favor, or a vague sense of *noblesse oblige*, or perhaps boredom. But I am serious. If you need help dealing with...*them.*" He rolled his eyes. "Call me." He handed me a scrap of paper with a number.

Did I trust him? I looked into his eyes and saw the slightest edge that only comes from having nothing. No, he got it. Maybe some of the royals, did, too. "Thank you, sir. I really appreciate it."

"And watch out for His Royal Highness Frederik. He is up to something."

"I know," I said.

11

MONEY

My mind replayed what had happened as I shaved the next morning. I wanted to regret what I said, and I knew I should, but I didn't. The only thing I regretted was that they might leave the Foundation.

And I still needed their money, damn it.

Damn everything.

A sharp pain brought me back to reality, and I looked to see blood running down my chin. Great.

I remembered quite well the first time I shaved—Dad had promised to teach me, but that night he couldn't even hold the razor steady and Mom had to show me. Then, weeks later, we had run out of razor blades. So I used a knife.

I ran my finger along the very faint scar on my neck. By the grace of God it was only a shallow cut. Dad promised he would buy me more disposable razors when he went to Memphis, but every time he did he "forgot." Kyle eventually found me some.

I closed my eyes, leaning against the mirror. Dad constantly made promises. Of the ones he wasn't too drunk to fulfill, he spent all the necessary money on alcohol instead. The only Christmas presents he had ever gotten me were things he found at the thrift store.

But he would promise anything. I would read online of the latest toys, the latest games, the latest shows, the latest everything, and know that I could never afford even one, and knew Dad wouldn't afford them either. I pirated for a bit, until I admitted it was wrong. When the Witch-Queen reformed copyright so I could legally download most old entertainment, it was like the Christmas I always wanted, brought to me by the Antichrist.

And then...

And then I had met the so-called Antichrist in person. And she gave me enough money to buy anything I could imagine. I could have Christmas every day for the rest of my life.

I opened my eyes and looked into the mirror. Who looked back?

A poor man? Hell, no. Not any more.

A noble in all but title? Over my dead body.

But what difference was there between me and Lynn's "friends?" If I had traveled back through time and visited Lumberton as I was now, past me would have not cared what the world called me. Only that I could buy whatever I wanted.

"Past me," I said out loud. No, the Michael Mason who knew nothing of real money was dead. Even if Lynn—God forbid—dumped me tomorrow, I would always know what it was like to insert a credit card into a reader and spend more in one transaction than I made in a year as a lumberjack.

But who now lived?

A poor man? A noble?

Her Imperial Majesty's boyfriend?

Me?

I sighed and washed my face. Whatever the case, I had done wrong. Confession would help.

"Bless me, Father, for I have sinned. It's been a week since my last confession. I completely lost my temper at... some business associates... and I took the Lord's name in vain twice. As I screamed at them."

"I see. Did you apologize?"

"Yes. And I apologized to someone I, uh, punched earlier. It's been a rough month."

"Young man, is this an ongoing thing?" Fr. Xavier asked.

"We hate each other, but I'm trying not to."

"That's a start. Are you at least *sorry?*"

"Sometimes?"

"The good news is, you only need attrition, fear of punishment, in this confessional. God brings you the rest of the way."

"Oh, I fear punishment, what with God not leaving those who take his name in vain unpunished. I also want to be the sort of person who doesn't lose his temper on people who don't... well, don't *completely* deserve it."

"'Do not let the sun go down on your anger.' If you allow your temper to simmer, it will eventually boil over. So I would like you to pray a complete rosary for this individual you're upset with, and be sure to pay attention when you say 'Hallowed be thy name.'"

"Yes, sir."

"Now will you make your Act of Contrition?"

"Oh my God, I am heartily sorry..."

I was on my fourth decade, kneeling by the Mary altar, when I heard a gasp. I swiveled my head to see the other parishioners disturbed by the presence of Her Imperial Majesty, and Her Imperial Majesty disturbed by the other parishioners. "Remain as you are!" she called. "No need to kneel!"

Some stood, some knelt anyway, and everyone looked awkward.

I waved her over, then resumed praying. "...especially those in most need of your mercy," I finished. "'Sup, Lynn."

She looked horribly out of place, her lips curled in a confused expression as she looked around her. "Are you OK?" she asked. "I was wondering when you'd come out."

"I didn't know you were waiting for me."

"Oh. Yeah. I guess I can't spoil the surprise. When you're done..." She frowned, puzzled.

"It'll be just a couple minutes," I promised.

"I'll wait, then." She stood beside me.

A couple minutes later, I crossed myself and kissed the crucifix. My mom had made the rosary herself, one of her Christmas gifts. She had never promised anything big, but she had always delivered.

Lynn kissed me on the cheek then followed me out.

"I'm glad you didn't ask people to, uh..."

"Kneel to *me* in their place of worship?" Lynn asked. "Heck, no, I wouldn't ask. One, it's seriously bad karma, if there is such a thing as karma. Two, it will instantly get blown out of proportion as an assault on religious freedom and I'll be having riots within twenty-four hours. Third..."

"Third?" I asked, blessing myself with holy water from a font.

Lynn watched me, puzzled again, then whispered in my ear. "My mom read this one story to me as a kid, about a prince who rules the world. He tries to conquer heaven with flying ships. Then God strikes him down with a mosquito. Seems like a reasonable lesson in humility, don't you think?"

"Sounds like it." The weather was cool outside, fall approaching. I didn't dare broach why Lynn was talking about family—as far as the rest of the world knew, she had emerged autochthoniously from the Moon.

"It was the one story she knew. I don't know why she picked *that* one to learn." She shrugged. "But she liked it. And I did, too."

We walked in silence for a time.

"So, this surprise?" I asked.

"Oh, yeah! It's supposed to be for Coronation Day, but I had to get it started already, so I guess it's an early Coronation Day present."

Lynn's attempt to replace all religious holidays with secular holidays on unrelated dates received very strong and very mixed reactions. Some people objected to the calendar reform in general, and celebrated the old holidays for the hell of it, sometimes violently. I thought it was kind of a good thing, since Christmas was no longer a big commercial celebration. Besides, it had gotten increasingly difficult to figure out what the old calendar dates would even be on the new calendar without an app, to the point where I had forgotten about it altogether.

St. John said that the Antichrist would think to change times and seasons. Just like Lynn did.

I glanced at her, savoring her beauty. St. John never said anything about this. Maybe her detractors were all wrong.

"A centimark for your thoughts?" Lynn asked me.

"Just thinking about calendar reform."

"Thinking what?" Lynn's voice dropped.

"That, uh, it was controversial."

Her eyes bored into me. "I know *that.*"

"I thought it was a good idea, sort of," I said.

She seemed relieved. "It's so much better, right?"

"I mean, it's *sort of—*"

I had never seen Lynn flip between peace and anger and back so quickly. "It's better," she said.

"Can we talk about something else?" I asked. "Oh, yeah, I need to get you a Coronation Day present, don't I?"

Lynn grinned ear to ear. "I should probably get two for you, since I'm going to be spoiling one."

Lynn took me to an elevator in the Palace, and we zoomed up. I followed her to a security checkpoint. The guards bowed as we passed through. Or passed up, because beyond the bullet-proof glass was a curve that just went... up.

"Come on," Lynn said calmly, walking to it, then up it.

"Right," I said, and followed until suddenly the cloudy sky was forwards, beyond Lynn's apartment. Beyond the railings on the side the sea was sideways.

This is crazy, I thought, and my stomach agreed. "Why on Earth did you build this, Lynn?"

"I needed the gravity generators to attract high-rank daemons, and they'd just be lying around most of the time," Lynn said. "Besides, a great view, isn't it?"

"Yeah." I tried not to look at it. "A great view."

We came to a curve leading to the disk in the center, where the high-level daemonology was supposed to happen, but we kept going up. Or forwards? A very confused bird flew overhead.

Walk, walk, walk. "What happens if the generator breaks?"

"Oh, if they blow, the whole Palace gets spaghettified," Lynn said. "But they're safe. All sorts of backups and backups to the backups."

"What about sabotage?"

"Everything is constantly watched by my daemons. There's not much point for anyone to try. Worst case scenario, my daemon phases me out before the waves hit me. Don't worry about it, Mike."

I had heard a different story before: the Witch-Queen had set up the Capital with artifical gravity so that a daemonic battle would kill everyone in it, creating a metropolis of living shields. But I didn't bring up that rumor. "I'm not worried about it," I said awkwardly. "I'm just—"

"Just what?"

"Never mind. Pretty cool, if weird."

We took another curve at Lynn's apartment, now back to normal gravity, and came to a glorious glass door, shining in colors through prisms. Lynn waved at it, and it opened for us. "Tada!" she said.

No, wait, that wasn't a glass door, that was a *diamond* door.

Diamonds studded the furniture inside the huge foyer, or even made up the furniture. Diamonds refracted light in the windows and made patterns along the black carpet. Diamonds, along with other jewels, decorated the otherwise bare mahogany walls. Diamonds jutted out of the wooden railing of the stairs and large diamond plates made up the stairs.

"I really need to show you around one day," Lynn said, as we passed through massive room after massive room. One room had an armchair with a stack of aged *tankoubon*, manga compilation books, on a table next to it. Aside from that, it didn't seem as if she actually lived here. "Actually, aside from Alice and a few of the old guard, I don't think I've shown this to anyone."

"It's pretty amazing," I told her.

She beamed. "Thanks."

We entered a dining room, and sat at the diamond table, whose edges reflected the open light just perfectly. A stapled sheet of papers with a pen lay on the table, the second ordinary thing I had seen in here.

"I'm making us lunch right now. It'll be a few minutes, but here's your surprise." Lynn slid the papers in front of me.

"It's in Japanese, Lynn," I said.

"Yeah, well, you probably know enough to figure out what this is."

I looked. "*Sekai no Iudex* something *anime* second something..." Wait, no... "Second season?"

"Yep!" Lynn said. "It's an Imperial Grant. I even dug up descendants of the original cast and staff. They're all thrilled."

Sometimes I forgot that Lynn was the Imperatrix Mundi. "Uh... wow."

"And here's the best part," she flipped through the papers to an empty signature line.

"*Maiku... Meisun?*" I read. "Oh, wait, I'm on the staff?"

"You're an executive producer!" Lynn's smile gleamed.

"I... I... whoa," I said.

"C'mon!" she said, handing the pen to me.

"I, uh..."

Lynn frowned. "What's wrong?"

What's *wrong*? Because I was the Witch-Queen's boyfriend, my favorite shows got uncanceled—

Though I didn't say anything, I could see by Lynn's look she had read me like a book. "Mike," she said. "Are you going to have another problem with money?"

"It's not that," I said.

"Then what is it?"

"I'm... I'm just surprised."

"Isn't this what you wanted?" she asked.

"Yes, well, I didn't expect to actually get it!"

"You have money, Mike. *I* have money. We can have what we want from now on."

I could feel something simmer within me. I forced myself to turn the temperature down. "I'm... I'm fine," I said. "Do I need to sign in Japanese?"

"Cursive English is fine."

I signed. There were several more places, but by the end my signatures were smooth. "Are you going to do this for other anime?" I asked.

"I don't know. I might make a general grant. I'm sure the industry will be revived if there's a few big hits."

"Good." Of course, which anime got remade would have more to do with Lynn than—nope, nope, nope, turn down the heat. Isn't this what I wanted?

Better to change the subject.

Lynn 'picked up the phone' with her empty hand. "This is Lynn," she frowned. "Yes. I see. Tell me if it gets worse. Bye."

"What's going on?"

"An independence movement in Chicago," Lynn said. "So far no revolutionary activity, but a possible breeding ground for it. We're trying to calm them down, but it's not working so well. And that's all I can say."

"OK," I said.

Invisible hands brought in an oven tray, half pizza, half breadsticks. My stomach rumbled. "If you're hungry after this, I've got all sorts of stuff in my fridges," Lynn said.

"Bless us, O Lord, and these thy gifts..." I prayed. Then I sampled the breadsticks. Great, but clearly homemade. Well, homemade by beings from beyond our brane. "I didn't know you had daemon-made food."

"Oh, I have human chefs, too, but today was a home cooking day," Lynn said. "A five percent chance, obviously, but life's not life without ups and downs."

"Five percent?"

"I roll a d20. Sometimes a d100 if I feel like it."

"Lynn, do you roll dice to avoid poison, or...?"

Lynn sighed. "Life can get too regular if you do the same thing too often. And yes, the less of a routine I have, the harder it is for someone to murder me."

"Huh," I said. I sampled some of the pizza—it was really good.

"There..." Lynn paused. "On the Moon, I only had a few flavors to choose from, and a few tables. I just rolled to pick at random every day."

I could sense, just barely, Lynn holding back an immense tide of loneliness. What to say? Could I say anything? I reached over and squeezed her hand.

"Yeah," Lynn said. "I almost never go back up. Just once a year."

"Why?"

"That's a secret," she said. "Anyway, after we're done eating, want me to show you around?"

"Sure."

I was not normally the sort of person who would engage in house-envy, but Lynn had a swank place—a library, a wine cellar, a pool, massive bathrooms, an AV room, multiple sun decks, and an office. Some locked doors were covered with inscriptions. Lynn didn't open those.

Then we went outside to the top observation deck, and I followed Lynn to the railing. I saw the whole city laid out before us, even the Basilica and the Needle's Eye, dwarfed at our height. I could even see the rail bridge back to what had once been Italy.

"Wow."

"Sometimes," Lynn said. "I come up here to see how big the Empire is. Because this is only a tiny part of it."

"Do you ever feel... small?" I asked.

She shook her head. "I'm the only one in this whole world qualified to do this. Without me... things would be bad again."

What would life be without the Witch-Queen?

What would life be without *Lynn?*

Lynn 'picked up her phone' again. "Yes. *Great.* I'll be there immediately." She hung up. "Sorry, Mike, I have to go. Just head straight out, would you? There's some dangerous stuff here."

"I'll walk straight out, promise," I said.

"Good. *Ikimashou.*" She snapped her fingers and was gone.

On my walk back to my apartment I nearly broke down.

Lynn was right.

I could have *anything* I wanted.

Even as something as completely insane as a new season of an anime.

I sat on a bench. Others, others who wouldn't think twice of spending anything they wanted on themselves, walked from building to building, or rode the trolley. Why couldn't I be like them?

But what if I *became* like them?

My phone rang. I pulled it out, wishing I had Lynn's magic hand-phone. "Yes?"

It was Johnson. "Ah, Mr. Mason, we have a bit of a problem."

Oh no. "What?" I asked.

"Some of the donors are having second thoughts. We did another survey of the possible sites, and it's going to take a lot more money to build in the Scandinavian Dominion."

"Then let's just build in NAWD, as we originally suggested."

"They're not interested in that. One said he didn't want to make things too nice for those who won't work."

I held my tongue.

"To be frank, I suspect His Royal Highness Frederik is behind this."

"Oh, I'm sure he is," I said. "Let me—" Peter Reiner! He could sort this out. "I'll see what I can do to get more donors onboard."

"Of course, sir."

We exchanged pleasantries, and disconnected. I groaned, holding my face. Great. Now I didn't have *enough* money.

Damned if I did, damned if I didn't.

I texted Peter Reiner.

`Hey, can I talk to you in person about the Mason Foundation? Something came up.`

A minute later, I got a reply.

`I'm available for thirty minutes on Tuesday at 3:00 PM NAECD time.`

I quickly texted him back.

Sounds like a plan.

Then I called Alice.

"Yes?"

"How do I get to New York tomorrow?"

"I'd call Omnitaxi. You can afford the supersonic class."

That Tuesday, I stood atop one of the Palace's landing pads, and with some trepidation, dialed the famous Omnitaxi number.

They picked up instantly. "Omnitaxi, from Anywhere to Anywhere. Where are you going?"

"New York, New York, 1 DaemonBusiness Plaza," I said. "I'd like the supersonic option."

"Where are you currently?"

"The Palace. In the Capital, I mean."

"Your name, sir."

"Michael Mason."

"Ah, we'll be right there."

They weren't kidding. Within five minutes the white aircar had landed in front of me. I hopped inside.

"Hello, sir!" the driver said brightly. "Be sure to strap yourself in completely, because we'll be going fast."

I made sure I was in, tight. "Uh, how do I pay?"

"Just insert your card right here," she said, extending a reader.

I put it in.

Then realized I didn't know how much I was spending.

Then realized I didn't *care* how much I was spending, anymore.

It had become reflexive.

What had happened to me?

"Here we GO!"

My stomach protested as we zoomed off.

I had been increasingly nervous as we traveled, and only became more nervous as I walked into the central skyscraper of 1 DaemonBusiness Plaza. I had done a little research on Peter Reiner while waiting, and found he had not one, but seven businesses in his holding group.

I composed myself on the way up. I would not beg. I would bring to his attention the situation, and he... and he would just fix it for me?

Really?

Calling Peter Reiner's office spartan barely covered it. He had a large mahogany desk with a laptop and a landline. One wall had a clock. One wall had a window showing the great view. And another held framed documents—stock certificates, portions of contracts, and newspaper articles.

The man himself was waiting behind the desk. He folded his newspaper and set it down. "Admiring the decor?" he asked me.

"Are those your successes?"

"No. Failures."

I looked closer. The stock certificates had lines slashed through the daemonic inscriptions to render them inactive. Contracts had clauses highlighted. One of the newspaper clippings read "Famed Black Entrepreneur Files for Bankruptcy." And one frame contained a rejection letter to the Washington Magisterial College.

I turned away. "That's... an interesting choice of reminders."

"Poignant, isn't it?" Peter Reiner asked. "I already have enough reminders of success. But please, take a seat."

I sat on the chair. "Frederik is moving against me."

"Yes, I suspected such would happen. And what are you going to do about it?"

"Other donors are reluctant to spend more on the Scandinavian site, and they don't want to build in NAWD, either."

"That's all very important to know, but what are you going to do about it?"

"...I don't know."

"Might I suggest that you stop holding your fellow donors at a distance and attend their parties, invest in their businesses, and in short, befriend them?"

I took a deep breath. No, I would not lose my temper. "I'm not their peer."

"Then, pray tell, why should they treat you as one? Or even look up to you?"

No, don't explode. "I guess they have no reason to," I said. "But I'm not going to schmooze with some rich..." I facepalmed.

"Mike—can I call you Mike?" he asked.

"Yes."

"Call me Peter." He waved at the window. "Let me ask you a question: if I offered you a million IM to jump out of there with a bungee-cord, would you?"

"Hell, no."

"What would you do for a million IM?"

I thought about it. "Well..."

"Would you pet a kitten?"

"I... guess. I'd assume there was a catch."

"There is no catch. It's just some crazy rich old lady who loves cats."

"I... well..."

He gave me a firm look. "The fact that you hesitate means it's not about the bungee-jump or the kitten. It's about the million IM."

"I don't believe in free money," I said.

"Really? Then what is the purpose of the Mason Foundation?"

I held my face.

"Believe me," Peter said. "I have no shortage of feelings about the old welfare system. Everyone I knew growing up was poor, and everyone thought that that was the way of things."

"Lynn said that you grew up on the street."

"No," he said immediately. "I grew up in a single-parent home, and when my mom died I ended up on the street. I swore that one day, I would own a mansion so large I had to have a team of maids clean it for me."

"Did you?"

"Eventually. But therein lies the difference: I *wanted* money, but you don't. Or perhaps you do, but don't want to admit it."

"I don't know. It seems everything was fine in my life until I..." Met Lynn? "Well, fell into money."

He raised an eyebrow. "You fell into it? It was just lying in a big pile in the street and you tripped over it?"

"I didn't *earn* it," I said. "It's from Lynn, or, well, I gambled and won."

"So you had a windfall. Random chance, in more ways than one," he said.

"Basically. I got lucky."

"And this is wrong because...?"

"It's not fair."

He sat back. "Let me tell you about fairness.

"Each day one of my cashiers, one of my managers, one of my magister-franchisees, and I all go to work. The cashier makes minimum wage of 8 IM an hour, more if the local jurisdiction raised it. The manager makes approximately 50,000 IM a year, or 200 an day, or 25 an hour. The magister-franchisee makes easily 150,000 to 250,000 a year net. I make about 500 IM per second, even if I did nothing. But all of us work the same day, or perhaps a little more."

He paused. "Is this fair?"

"Not really," I said.

"Why not?"

"Because you didn't work any harder than the cashier."

"Perhaps. But you can't judge simply on the basis of time, or even of physical effort. The cashier goes home and plays videogames when he's done. My work has become my entire life. I even dream about it. But let me tell you the real difference between me and the cashier: capital. You were a lumberjack, correct?"

"Yes," I said.

"Did you own a chainsaw?"

"Yeah, so?"

"Did you do more work with the chainsaw than if you had used a hatchet, or your bare hands?"

"Duh. Why?"

"So isn't that unfair? Shouldn't you only use a hatchet, to be fair to those who don't have chainsaws? A flint one, of course, to be fair to the neolithic lumberjacks who didn't even have metal."

"...Oh."

"You see, people think of capital as money. But it could be anything: skills, connections, land, a tool, a government license, intellectual property. Anything. If capitalism is unfair because I have money and you don't, so is using a chainsaw that you own and I don't."

"A business empire is worth a lot more than a chainsaw, though."

"Yes, and a chainsaw costs 100 IM to replace. I once lost 6 billion IM in a month. I have to say, it brought to mind the fleetingness of worldly wealth."

I held my head. What he was saying made sense, but it also somehow *didn't* make sense.

"But, sure, let's say someone overthrows your girlfriend, and, angered by her laissez-faire policies, imposes a communist dictatorship and redistributes money equally. Then let's say he gets overthrown next, and we're back to capitalism. What happens?"

"I don't know. I suspect you're going to say that things still wouldn't be 'fair.' Some people would be rich and others poor."

"The *same* people will become rich and the *same* people will become poor. With some variation, of course. 'It takes some fortune to make a fortune', as

I like to say. But the reason I am *here.*" He tapped the desk. "Is because I was *there.*" He pointed to the wall of failures. "I won't pretend this is solely because of my own skill and work. But I was the one who was willing to learn the skills and do the work, over and over again, until the luck fell into place."

"I see," I said, unsure what else to say.

"Mike, I don't know how much money you made, but I've known people who started business empires from a 1,000 IM Imperial Business Bureau microloan. You can do all of that out of your own pocket. Maybe you don't want to put in the work. Maybe you'd rather stay a lumberjack, or just be the Imperatrix's boyfriend. But the Empire leveled the playing field. There is nothing legally stopping you from doing whatever you want with your money."

"Maybe it would be one thing if I had earned this," I argued, "But I didn't. It was pure chance."

"Perhaps so. My point is that where the money comes from is less important than what you do with it. And what you do with it has the most to do with who you are."

"I tried to give it away."

"And evidently that's not working," Peter said, meeting my eyes.

"So, what, start a side hustle?"

"If that's too much work, invest in index funds or Imperial bonds. Or a hedge fund. Or real estate. The truth is, Mike, the only difference between us is that I chose to pursue a business empire and you didn't. Some thirty years ago, even minimum wage would have been a massive improvement in my circumstances. So no matter how little money you made as a lumberjack, you lived in America. You could have learned the skills to go into business and done so."

I felt my temper rise, opened my mouth, then closed it. No, whether I agreed fully or not, he had a point. There had been nothing stopping me from leaving Lumberton and trying to find a job in a big city. I only stayed home because...

"I'm not going to question why," Peter said. "We all have our own issues. But dare I say that projecting those issues onto other people is not going to help."

"Right," I agreed.

"So how about this? I have another meeting to go to in five minutes, but I can get you in on a meet-and-greet at the Daemonic Manufacturing Tradeshow. There are multiple daemonic construction companies. Talk to them and see if you can get something worked out for the Foundation. Or, if nothing else, step a foot into a world that you don't understand and see what it's like."

"Thanks."

"You're welcome. A pleasure talking to you."

"Mine as well," I said.

I stepped back out into the noise and lights of New York City. I could almost feel old grief in the cold air. Lynn had taken this as one of her first cities outside of Italy, and in the process thousands had died. After that, she turned the screws carefully, trying to coerce people to surrender to her with money rather than machine guns.

My head spun for other reasons. Peter had a point: if using what you had to make money was wrong, then I had sinned the moment I bought my own chainsaw. And...

And if it hadn't been for Mom, I would have left Lumberton long ago. Just gone to a city and tried to make a living somehow.

"It's still not fair." I said out loud. The nobles hadn't earned anything—the Witch-Queen had just dumped money and power on them. But neither had I. The Witch-Queen had *also* dumped money on me, if not so much power, and now...

Now, maybe it was time to think about money differently. I could invest it somehow. Or, heck, maybe start something so I'd have something to do with my time. I didn't *have* to give it away.

Later, though. If I thought any more about money right now, my brain was going to explode.

I got into the Omnitaxi. "Can we change course?"

"Sure thing," she said. "Where to?"

"There's a refugee camp in the Tennessee Subdominion. Could you take me there?"

"Yep. From Anywhere to Anywhere!"

The night had only grown colder when we arrived. I decided I would have to stay the night. Hopefully someone would have a spare sleeping bag.

I looked around with new eyes. Yes, everyone here had been screwed accidentally or on purpose by the Witch-Queen, or events, or their own unwillingness to accept change. And here I was, still wearing a suit after my meeting. Maybe this wasn't fair.

But it was how the world worked.

You know what? I'd go see Mom, and we'd talk about Dad. Then maybe the pain wouldn't be so bad. Maybe I could even convince Lynn to let us visit his grave in Lumberton's small cemetery.

Maybe she'd come, too. I could explain why we were the way we were, and how we could—I froze.

Beyond the edge of the old tents, where my village had been, were only tent pegs and the remains of fireplaces.

12

INTRIGUE

A plot?

A daemonic attack?

Dear God *no!*

My hands were shaking as I dialed Lynn.

"Mike? What's up?"

"This is an emergency!" I shouted. "My village is gone!"

"Give me five seconds."

A few moments later, Lynn appeared with a whoosh. She wore sturdy clothes and a sharp look in her eyes. She looked around, concern growing.

"Where are they?" I asked. "We have to find them!" Thoughts raced through my mind.

"Mike," Lynn said. "Match my breathing." She breathed in slowly, then breathed out. I followed as best I could, until I felt a bit calmer.

"Why are you here?" Lynn asked. "Did you come to visit?"

"I was in New York for a meeting and decided to visit," I said. "And this is what I found." Tension rose in my shoulders, but I tried to stay calm.

"Did they call you?"

I checked my phone log. No calls, no texts. "They didn't contact me."

"Have you tried calling them?" Lynn asked.

I got out my phone and dialed Kyle.

"Hello, you've reached the voice mail of Kyle Franklin. I'm unable to take your call right now. Please do not leave a message. BEEP."

I hung up.

"*Don't* leave a message?" Lynn asked.

"He thinks the government spies on the voicemail system."

Lynn rolled her eyes. "We don't have that kind of time on our hands."

"Listen, whatever, we need to find them." I texted Mom.

Mom, where are you? Please reply right away.

No reply.

"*Kyle Franklin ikiteiru ka?*" Lynn asked the air, then looked at me. "He's still alive. Give me more names."

I listed them off my phone, trying their numbers, too.

No one answered, but they were all still alive, according to Lynn.

"Can you tell where they are?" I asked Lynn.

"No," she said. "But I know they're still alive. Let's go."

I tried breathing as Lynn had showed me on our way to the center of the camp. Lynn pulled out her gravity mapper, and gave orders in Japanese. In the night around us, the air became hazy.

"Can you find them with that?" I asked.

"No. The most powerful gravity mappers in the world can't track people for more than a few miles. My concern is that whoever did this probably set this up as a trap for either me or you."

I shut up.

The door of the office was locked. Lynn glanced at her mapper and led me to another building. Then slammed the corrugated metal so hard the building rang.

"Stay next to me," Lynn said.

I glanced at her face. I saw an edge I had only seen her once before, when she had sprung me from the jail in Monaco.

The door opened to show the commandant, who gasped at the sight of us. "Your Imperial Majesty!"

"Where are the displaced persons from Lumberton?" Lynn demanded calmly.

He turned pale. "Ma'am, a group of magisters from the Mason Foundation came and—"

"What the *hell?*" I shouted. "We don't even have magisters!"

"Let's all calm down," Lynn said, squeezing my hand. "They said they were from the Mason Foundation?"

"Yes, ma'am. They had documentation."

My head was spinning.

"And what did they do?"

"They arrived with a bunch of airbuses and took them to the Memphis Processing Center. They had the documentation all in order. Please, Your Imperial Majesty, I had nothing to do with this!"

I saw calculations pass over Lynn's face. "Stay there. Cooperate with the SMP."

"Yes, ma'am!"

Lynn walked off, and I followed her. "I didn't do this!" I protested.

"I know you didn't, dear," Lynn said. She 'picked up the phone.' "Mike's village was moved, and the commandant claims the Mason Foundation did it. Find out. I'm heading to Memphis. Yes. Good. Get to it.'" She 'hung up.'

"Memphis?" I asked.

"We'll find out pretty quickly if there's a paper trail," Lynn said. "How did you get here?"

"Omnitaxi."

"Take it to the Ducal Palace of Memphis. I'll meet you there."

I tried to pray the rosary, but I could barely concentrate. We arrived almost immediately at the duke's countryside estate.

The Ducal Palace was fancy, though quaint compared to what I had seen in the Capital. It was only three stories and painted with gold.

The airpads were crowded with expensive cars. Lynn was waiting, in even fancier clothes than before. She chanted names as she paged through a folder. Everyone in Lumberton hated Duke Edgeworth, but in that moment I truly understood he was only one of over two thousand dukes in the whole Empire. Lynn had to look him up. She closed the folder and it vanished. "He has no dirty laundry. But that doesn't mean anything."

"The duke has expensive habits," I said, looking around. "But that doesn't mean he has taste."

"Tell me about it," Lynn said. We went up to the gilded gates where a party of liveried doormen awaited with concern. "Out of the way," Lynn said. She snapped her fingers and daemons with hazy outlines appeared around her.

The doormen broke out into two lines and stood at attention as we walked in. "Your Imperial Majesty, His Grace is eagerly waiting your pleasure," said a butler, opening the door.

Lynn didn't respond, walking straight on through. "Be careful," she told me.

I looked around. The interior was no less tacky than the outside. I felt revulsion at all the gaudy decor—things we had slaved to pay for, but which did nothing but serve as shiny things for the duke to enjoy.

But right now I would give him all of it all over again if he could find my friends and family.

We entered the dining room. Lynn snapped her fingers and more daemons formed a hazy ring around us.

Duke Edgeworth himself sat behind the ornate table on a massive chair that barely fit his girth. He got up with effort and bowed. "Your Imperial Majesty, to what do I owe the pleasure of your visit?"

"Lumberton is missing," Lynn said.

"Lumberton?"

"The village I've ordered you to keep an eye on."

"Ah. I've cooperated with the investigation fully, of course—"

"Do you have *any* idea what I'm talking about?"

The Duke stopped. "Well, er, ma'am, this is about the daemonic infestation?"

"This is about how someone kidnapped my village," I said, holding back my fury like an angry dog on a leash.

"I knew nothing of this!" The Duke said. "Of course I will cooperate fully with the investigation—"

"Edgeworth, I am not interested in excuses," Lynn said. "I want to know if you have *any information* on this."

"I can find—"

"Any information *right now.*"

"I have to admit this is the first I've heard of the situation but—"

"Where did the buses go?"

"The what?"

"If you know nothing, then you've failed at your job."

The duke shut up.

"If you want to stay here, *do* cooperate with the investigation. The SMP will be here shortly."

"Yes, of course, Your Imperial Majesty, if you would just—"

But Lynn was already walking out. I followed her.

Outside, I could see the stars. "Lynn, are you going to punish him?"

"Maybe. People who screw up on the job don't get to keep it." Lynn looked up. "It doesn't matter if he *does* know, only that he should have known. But that's my business."

"Your Imperial Majesty!" the duke cried, stumbling after us. He breathed deeply. "There—there was a missive from the King of Washington."

Lynn swiveled. "Oh?"

"He wanted my authorization for a number of change of jurisdiction forms."

Lynn turned and raised an eyebrow. "How many?"

"About a thousand five hundred."

"What did you do with them?"

"I filled them out and sent them back."

"Who was the sponsor?" I asked.

"Some foundation, I can find out—"

"And where was the new jurisdiction?" Lynn asked.

"I don't remember."

I felt sick.

"Find out immediately," Lynn said. "And if I meet you again, don't remember important information *later*."

"Yes, Your Imperial Majesty!"

"Mike, head to Washington D.C. I'll be there soon."

I finished the rosary, or tried, by the time we arrived. I figured Mary would get the situation, even if I couldn't concentrate.

Washington D.C. had been badly damaged in the War. Most of it had been leveled, and thousands, including the President, had perished.

The King of Washington had set up shop in a neighborhood near the wreck of the Capitol Mall. He had been some senator who had managed to be the surviving government leader to surrender. His palace was made of white marble, as if to convince us all that he was the legitimate ruler of his chunk of America.

The thought threw me for a moment. Didn't I consider *Lynn* the true ruler of the world now?

The true ruler of the world was once again waiting for me, looking through another folder and chanting more names. "According to the SMP, there are between fourteen to eighteen scandals that King George is somehow involved in. None of them deeply affected the government per se, and he was doing a good job, so I had decided to leave him in power. But that ends today if he doesn't have a good explanation for this."

Men in suits opened the doors for us, and magisters looked on Lynn's daemonic army warily. Lynn looked straight ahead. Her expression had gotten harder.

The King was waiting for us in his study. He wore an elaborately embroidered robe, as naturally as if he had never worn a senator's suit. He bowed to Lynn. "Your Imperial Majesty, what can I do for you?"

"A village is missing. Did you have anything to do with this?"

"No, ma'am," he said without skipping a beat.

"Why did you ask for a thousand five hundred change of jurisdiction forms from the Duke of Memphis?"

He pulled out a smartphone and dialed a number. "Abel? Get here immediately, it's Imperial business."

Lynn seemed mildly pleased.

"Do you want anything while you wait? Wine?"

I almost yelled at him for offering wine when my village was in danger, but I held my tongue. Lynn glanced at my face. "No," she said. "But do bring us water."

"Of course. James, do bring us some water."

A man in a less fancy suit entered and bowed to us. "Your Imperial Majesty, Your Majesty."

"Did we send for a thousand change of jurisdiction forms?" the King asked.

"Sir, we process tens of thousands every day."

"From Memphis, to all sorts of other places?" I asked.

He raised an eyebrow. "Sir," he said, exasperated. "Memphis is not even in one of our subdominions."

"Yet, nonetheless, you asked for one thousand five hundred of them," Lynn said icily.

"Ma'am, the only reason we would need that was if the migrants were moving *to* one of our subdominions. They may have been Form I-994s, Supplemental Passport Information, from passing through our processing centers."

"Did we ask for them?"

"Sir, we process so many—"

"I don't care about your excuses!" Lynn shouted.

"Ma'am, we will find out as soon as we can. There are just so many of these documents."

Lynn paused. "Very well. George, you have my number. Call me as soon as you find out. Mike, let's go."

We walked out through the castle, me feeling all sorts of uneasy. I was already worried, but seeing Lynn explode like that made it all the worse.

"Mike, let's do some more box breathing, all right?" Lynn asked. "Four seconds each. In... Out..."

"I'm scared," I said.

"I know you are. But right now you should sleep. This is going to take some time, and the SMP needs time to hunt them down, too. So right now, I'm going to find you a hotel, and then you're going to go to bed."

"Lynn—"

"If you get upset, you'll start making mistakes."

Then why the hell did you shout at that poor bureaucrat? I didn't ask, because Lynn still had that edge in her eyes.

"Call me as soon as you have information," I said.

"I will." She gave me a hug. "I know how hard it is to lose people. I'll do anything to make sure you don't."

Kyle was running, running from daemons that ever shifted and had hooks instead of hands. But there were daemons everywhere, pursuing everyone I loved. If only we had more money, we could have paid the daemons off, but no matter how hard I argued with Peter he wouldn't just write us a check...

I woke up from a nightmare to find myself in a strange bed. Oh. Yeah. I was in that bed and breakfast Lynn had found for me.

What time was it? I felt all sorts of jet lag. I also felt sick to my stomach.

I found a suitcase with clothing in it and a note from Lynn.

`Text me when you're up. I have news. — Lynn, I.`
`M.`

I texted Lynn immediately.

What's going on?

Lynn appeared in a whoosh. "We found everyone."

"Thank God!" I said sincerely. "Is everyone all right?"

"Doing fantastic, actually. They all thank you for their new jobs."

"Their what?"

"Their new jobs," Lynn repeated. "They said you had sent some magisters three days ago saying you had a new settlement for all of them."

New worry flooded in to replace the old worry. "Where's the new settlement?!" I demanded.

"Nowhere. Whoever did this sent every family to a different city."

I fell back on the bed. "But they all have jobs?"

"Jobs, money, houses, even new cellphones," Lynn said. "The two people we couldn't find were your mom and your friend Kyle."

"Oh no," I said.

"Have you eaten?"

"I just woke up."

"Time for breakfast. They're safe for the moment, and we'll find out the truth soon enough."

"Right," I said. I was hungry.

We headed down to the brightly-lit dining room. People already sat at the various tables, laughing and talking, until they saw us. The room fell silent as Lynn and I walked to a table.

A shaking teenager waitress came up, staring at us. "What—what would you like to order?"

Lynn took the menu and rolled her dice. "Two bacon and cheese omelets and two cinnamon rolls. And two glasses of water!"

"Yes... ma'am..." she hurried off.

I considered trying to tell her Lynn wasn't so scary... but was she?

"How are you feeling?" Lynn asked.

"Scared," I said. "I'm so worried."

"We're making progress," she said. "Right now, I'm concerned about you. This is definitely an attack on you, which is also on me."

We waited in silence, Lynn calmly meeting my eyes. I tried that deep breathing and calmed a little. Why not wait? So far, everyone was safe and sound. So far.

"I can bring everyone back," Lynn said. "A change of jurisdiction is easy to reverse—"

"No!"

She raised an eyebrow.

"We've already had so much interference in our lives. Please, just leave us alone," I pleaded.

What was I even doing? Wasn't this what I wanted?

Because I knew in that moment that if Lynn didn't force us back together, the village of Lumberton was gone forever.

I held my face.

Lynn stroked my shoulder. "I won't. Promise. If this is what you want, I'll leave them all alone. But I will get you all in contact."

"Thank you."

The waitress came back with the platter. Then she dropped it, the plates shattering. "Oh. I'm sorry." She stared at Lynn.

Lynn met her eyes.

The waitress shook, but continued to stare.

"What do you think that accomplished?" Lynn asked.

"What is *wrong* with you!?" the waitress screeched. "Just waltzing back here after all you've done?"

"Sandy!" a balding man said, shoving his way through tables said. "For God's sake what are you—Your Imperial Majesty, I am very, very sorry—" But the fury in his voice was not directed at the waitress.

"Let's just eat somewhere else," I said.

"Why?" Lynn asked. "I'm sure accidents like that don't happen every time."

"Of course not," the manager said, and grabbed the waitress, wrenching her arm. She yelped, stumbling.

Lynn snapped her fingers. Invisible hands seized the manager, then slammed him through the tables into the wall. The waitress hit the floor. The manager struggled, but couldn't move.

"Lynn!" I shouted. "What the hell?"

Lynn wasn't listening. She walked up to the manager as the waitress watched in horror. "Don't. Hurt. Your. Employees," Lynn said with utter calm. "Not to please me. Not to please anyone else. Understood?"

"Of course, of course!" the manager squeaked.

"Good." Lynn returned to our table and sat down. The waitress ran out crying. The manager hurried out the opposite direction.

A older couple carried their plates to us. "Please. Just eat and leave us alone!"

"Perfect," Lynn said with a slight smile on her lips.

"Lynn?"

"What's wrong?"

"You..." But I saw something worse than anger in Lynn's eyes: satisfaction. I tried to say something, but nothing came out.

"Aren't you hungry?"

I looked at the food. Technically, Lynn hadn't stolen it. "Bless us, O Lord, and these thy gifts..." I prayed.

We ate in silence.

Back in our room, I asked, "Lynn, what the hell was that?"

"The curse of being the Witch-Queen," Lynn said. "It comes with the job."

That wasn't what I meant. But the longer this investigation had gone on, the *crueler* Lynn had acted. "What's going on with the investigation?" I asked, for lack of other words.

"Whoever did this had a lot of resources. More than your Mason Foundation."

"Your?"

"Yes, that's the strange thing. The paperwork was filed from a place called the Mason *Memorial* Foundation, a non-profit registered in Washington D.C. That explains why they needed all those forms."

Somewhere within a few miles, the people who had done this had their HQ. "We need to confront them."

"Already did. They just have an Imperial Post Box and an empty office. It's going to take some time to unravel. We should head home."

"I guess."

"The one thing I don't know is why the cellphones. To stop you from communicating, obviously, but—"

It hit me in one horrible instant. "Lynn!"

"Yes?"

"It's Prince Frederik of the Scandinavian Dominion."

She raised an eyebrow. *"What?"*

"Remember when we went to the Monte Carlo Casino and I got arrested?" I asked. "The phones were jammed then."

"What does that have to do with Prince Frederik?" she asked.

"I punched him in the face and he lost a tooth," I said.

She raised an eyebrow.

"Ever since, he's been out to get me," I said. "Please, Lynn, believe me."

Lynn looked thoughtful. "The Scandinavian Dominion does have a lot of wireless communications businesses. But this is a stretch, Mike."

"Please," I said. "Can we go confront him?"

She paused. "I've known Frederik for years, and I can't imagine him doing anything like this. But it is true we never tracked down who jammed the phones at Monte Carlo. Let's go."

The flight to Fredensborg, even on a supersonic aircar, took hours.

Had I just been imagining things? I knew Prince Frederik hated me, but this would be far even for him. Or would it?

But what would he get out of this? To destroy my home, yes, but *why?*

The Omnitaxi slowed as we approached the palace, a massive green-roofed structure. Though less fancy, it was huge compared to all the other palaces I had seen in the last twenty-four hours.

Lynn was waiting for me when we landed. She looked serious.

"Mike, the SMP unraveled the Mason Memorial Foundation while you were on your way. It was funded by a telecom giant in the Denmark Subdominion. I don't want to suspect Frederik, but this... this is evidence."

"Let's go," I said.

We walked up to the door and knocked.

A blond-haired butler poked his head out. "Your Imperial Majesty and Mr. Mason, His Royal Highness is expecting you."

We shared a look. Lynn had gotten instantly angrier, then calmer. "Let us in."

The guards watched my every moment as I walked through the historic halls. We came to a study. "Her Imperial Majesty and Michael Mason, sir," the butler announced.

"Please, enter."

We stepped in to see Prince Frederik turn from his desk, raising an eyebrow at me. "What brings you here?" he asked, perfectly calm.

"What the hell did you do to my village?"

"Oh, you finally found out?" he asked. "I did nothing that wasn't perfectly legal."

"*What?*"

"You see," he said. "I understand Imperial citizens in such a plight will seek any way out. And I gave them one." He folded his hands.

"You tore us apart!"

"Did you think I could arrange over a thousand well-paying jobs all in one settlement? Would you rather them remain cold, penniless, and homeless until you've got everything perfect?"

"You took our phones!"

"I offered them all new phones. It's not my fault if they don't remember their contacts without the SIM card. Do you?"

I opened my mouth, but barely held myself back from flooring him.

"Why?" Lynn asked calmly. "Why did you do this?"

"Proof."

"Proof?"

"That Mr. Mason here is by no means a fitting mate. Almost a month after he decides to act, he has done nothing more than hold meetings, beg for money, and scream at those from whom he's begging money. I changed his entire village's life in three days. And apparently he didn't even notice."

I took some deep breaths. No. I wouldn't floor the guy. I wouldn't give in.

"Why do you care?" Lynn asked.

"Because, Your Imperial Majesty, let it suffice to say that *I* seek your hand."

"What?" we asked.

"Consider," Prince Frederik said. "He is a worthless peasant who knows nothing of culture, has no competence when it comes to actual ruling, and is so full of anger that he has not once but twice exploded on your friends. I, on the other hand—"

"Shut up!"

"And again he can only rage—"

"You kidnapped my village!"

"On the contrary, they all willingly chose—"

"Then where is my mom?"

He hesitated.

"Where are they?" Lynn asked icily.

"Safe," Frederik said. "But why the care? Your 'boyfriend' has no taste, no culture, and if not for you, not even money. Whereas—"

"Skip the sales pitch," Lynn said.

"Very well. Consider, Your Imperial Majesty, the future. you will not live forever. One day a heir will sit on your throne. You will need someone to be that heir's father. Who would you rather it be, teaching your child how to reign in your place? A lumberjack from nowhere? Or a gentleman who knows how to wield power and money with more than platitudes and temper tantrums?"

"You know what?" Lynn asked. "Mike may be a nobody from nowhere. But unlike you, he actually cares for me as a person and not as a political alliance with a bonus uterus."

"I'm sure he wants to put his filthy—"

Lynn snapped her fingers.

Invisible hands lifted up the prince and slammed him high against the wall.

He reached for his throat, struggling.

"Lynn! Don't kill him!"

She looked at me, then snapped her fingers again. He crashed down to the ground. "Why?" she asked him. "How could you do such a thing? You ruined a thousand innocents lives just to get back—"

"I am trying to protect *you*," he said, gasping.

"Says the man who destroyed my village to get back at me!" I snapped. I could barely hold myself back.

"Not one of them is hurt. They are simply scattered."

"You tore them apart!"

"Again—"

"I don't care about your damn excuses."

I saw something move deep within Lynn, like an immense beast stirring awake. *"Letore do kache o kudasai,"* she said, and a clipboard appeared in her hand. She started writing.

I thought better of my next words. "Dude," I said instead.

"Do not call me *dude.*"

"Sir, we don't need to do this. Let's just call it quits here and now."

"With *you?*" he spat. "You can't even help your own village!"

"Yes, and you tore that village apart," Lynn said. The Imperial Seal appeared in her hand and she stamped the paper.

"Your Imperial Majesty," he said, watching her. "What in God's name do you see in him? He's just a commoner."

"Yes," Lynn said, and turned the clipboard around. "And now so are you."

His jaw just about hit the floor. "Excuse me—"

"Would you keep this individual detained until the SMP arrives?" Lynn asked the shocked guards. "I must be going."

"Lynn—" I started.

"Your Imperial Majesty, I—"

Lynn took my hand and tugged me along. "We're done here. And so is he."

13

Revenge

Outside, I looked back at Frederik's palace, still stately and unchanged. His *former* palace. Sure, I hated Frederik, but now he had lost his home, too. Was this really OK?

What was I talking about? He had a ton of money. He'd be fine, just humiliated.

"There's a bunch of loose ends I need to tie up here," Lynn said. "How about you head home?"

I saw into her eyes and still saw that horrible anger. What would she do after I left?

"I'll find your mom," Lynn promised. "His servants will know the truth. But even if *he* begs and pleads, I'm not reinstating him."

"Good," I said. "I'll head home."

"Dad, please. You said—"
 "Next week, Mike."
 "It's always next week."
 "This time for sure."

I looked at the bottle of booze in his hands. Without thinking I grabbed it and smashed it against the concrete.

Dad roared and grabbed me. "You brat!" He picked me up and threw me—then he was next to me. "I'm so sorry, Mike, I just—"

I woke up.

I felt my sweat-covered body. No bruises, no cuts.

Why *that* one? I hadn't had that nightmare in years.

Was it Lynn?

Lynn, who slammed a guy across a room for hurting a girl and nearly killed a former friend for hurting me?

I sighed. My head hurt. At least Lynn had gone berserk in protecting me, and not *at* me.

But was that it?

I shook my head. Better not to dwell on the past.

I shaved, showered, and checked the news.

"SCANDINAVIAN PRINCE ACCUSED OF CORRUPTION, EX-PELLED FROM ROYAL FAMILY."

"Dear God," I said out loud.

The pretty young reporter stood in front of the palace I had left last night. "According to a source within the Scandanavian Royal Family, Her Imperial Majesty revoked the former prince's titles over underworld ties..."

But that's *not* what happened!

"What have you done, Lynn?" I asked out loud.

Why not ask her?

I dialed her number.

"What's up, Mike? I have only five minutes."

"I saw on the news—"

"Not my problem."

"What?"

"They threw their own child under the bus. Who am I stop them?"

"Lynn, listen—"

"By the way, we found Kyle and your mom."

I shut up.

"Apparently the former prince had them secretly transferred to his subdominion and arrested on some pretext. Either he wanted them out of the way or he did it deliberately to get back at you. They're both OK, just shaken."

"Thank you," I said, breathing in relief.

"I offered your mom a place in the Capital. She'll be here tomorrow. Your friend wanted to go to Chicago to stay with his grandfather, so I gave him a ticket."

Yes. Because Lumberton was destroyed.

Sure, maybe we were all better off now. But Frederik had treated us if we were only enemy pawns on his chessboard. He probably had passed it off to a servant and signed a paper. And Lumberton ceased to exist.

Even then... no matter how much Frederik suffered for it, Lynn had torn his family apart, too.

I took a deep breath. "Lynn."

"What?"

"Give Frederik a second chance."

"What on Earth, Mike? After all he's done, you want to give *him* a second chance?"

"His family disowned him."

"That's not my business."

"It *is* your business, damn it! They're all afraid of you!"

Lynn fell silent.

"Please," I said. "At least give him a pardon. Don't give him power again, but at least let him be in contact with his family."

The line stayed silent.

"Please, Lynn. Please?"

"I'll think of something. Got to go."

"Thanks."

"Don't worry about it. Bye!"

I breathed a sigh of relief.

Mom climbed out of the Omnitaxi, and ran to me the moment she saw me. We hugged, holding on to each other as if we could make sure would never be parted.

We broke off. *Honey, you have no idea how glad I am to see you!* she signed.

I was so worried! I signed back. *Were you OK?*

No one there spoke English or ASL. But I made it through, thanks to Our Lady. They never said what they wanted.

It was a scheme by... a former prince.

I heard about our village.

Yeah. Lynn's supposed to get us all in contact. But here, let me get you settled in.

Lynn had found another apartment in my complex for her. All her stuff was already there, waiting in boxes. *What a pretty apartment,* Mom signed.

I have Dad's bottle cap, I signed.

I wonder what they thought of it.

I shrugged. *The SMP knows a ton. They probably know the truth.*

They can know it. I don't mind everyone knowing.

I heard a knock at the door. *Oh, yeah, I need to tell Lynn to get you a light-up doorbell.* I opened to find Lynn herself.

Morning everyone, she signed. *Mrs. Mason, I'm sorry things went this far. But you're safe now.*

Thank you so much, Mom signed.

You know ASL now? I signed back.

I told you I learn languages for fun. But I'm still learning.

I saw Mom sign in my peripheral vision. *Let me pull up a chair.*

Lynn muttered in Japanese and snapped her fingers. Armchairs and the couch arranged themselves in a triangle. *That should do.*

We sat down. *Is everyone all right?* Mom asked.

They only targeted you and Kyle. Everyone else is fine, just scattered.

I told Lynn not to try and force everyone back together, I signed.

That's the right decision, Mom signed. *How are you doing, Lynn? We've never had a chance to talk.*

I've just been busy. There's always a crisis or two ongoing, Lynn signed. *But we haven't made any progress on the tainted water SMT. The daemons just disappeared. Not that it matters to you at this point.*

It matters to the other villages.

Lynn nodded. *Yes. But until we find the mother daemon, I can't let anyone go back, for everyone's safety. But that's my business. The person responsible for your imprisonment has been punished. Which brings me to...* Lynn snapped her fingers and tickets flew out to us.

JUDGMENT GAMES VVIP ACCESS. Admit one.

What? I asked. *Oh. Sweet.* I had always wanted to see one in person, and now I knew exactly who I wanted to see humiliated.

You wanted to give him another chance. So I am. People can't publicly defy me without consequences.

You don't have to take me, Mom signed. *I've already forgiven whoever it was, and I'm not a fan of the games.*

It's all OK. Just wanted to offer.

Thanks, Lynn, I signed.

You're welcome.

But please, Lynn, tell me about yourself, Mom signed.

I was born to... a mother, Lynn signed. *Grew up in poverty. I discovered daemonology when I was young. Got in serious trouble, escaped, ran into a revolutionary movement. I got in even MORE trouble. Then the Magisterium killed most of us. I got out with... a friend. We wandered the world, joining whatever movements we could find. Eventually... our luck ran out. I escaped to the Moon. I prepared for two years, came down as the most powerful magister of all time, and the rest is history.*

I was surprised Lynn brought up so much detail. She hadn't even told *me* those details.

But what do you do with your spare time? That sort of thing.

Oh, that? I spend most of my time working, but I spend my free time reading or having fun with your son.

We also watch anime, I signed. Come to think of it, we hadn't done much but watch anime and talk.

We should get together and play video games some time, Lynn signed.

Sure thing.

Do you believe, Lynn? Mom signed.

I'm an atheist, Lynn signed. *But I don't object to anyone believing.*

You're always welcome to come to Mass with me, I signed.

Maybe one day I'll take you up on that. Lynn winked. Then she 'picked up the phone.' "I'm busy. What? I'll be right there." *Sorry, guys, I have to go right now. We found a lead, and I have to phase right over to see it myself. If I have free time afterwards, I'll text you, Mike. All right?*

You're always welcome to come over, Mom signed.

Sure thing, Lynn signed. "*Ikimashou*!" she said out loud. She snapped her fingers and was gone.

How long have you known her, Mike? Mom asked.

Just the three months, I signed. Had it been three months? I felt like I had always known her.

I like her and I love you, but I want you to be careful. Mom held up the ticket. *Someone who does cruel things to those she hates can do cruel things to those she loves.*

The Judgment Games are just harmless fun, Mom, I signed.

Really? Do the contestants feel the same way?

I stopped.

I was never comfortable with you watching them. Even if they are willing, even if some of them are criminals, I don't like to see people being hurt.

But they're potentially avoiding a prison sentence if they play, I signed. *And besides, Frederik did some horrible things to you...* My face fell at her expression.

Listen, the point isn't whether you like them or not, and the point isn't whether the contestants deserve it or not. The question is how Lynn feels about them, since she's the one who set them up and keeps them going. Is it about revenge? Sadism? Entertainment?

I don't know, I signed.

You need to find that out before you go deeper. You need to really know who she is before you start thinking about something more permanent. Yes, Mike, I can tell.

Good old mom telepathy.

Mom laughed. *I'm not saying you should break up. Just be sure you know what you're getting into before you get into it.*

I understand, Mom.

Good.

Lynn texted me an hour later saying she could meet me for tea in the garden.

I didn't know the Palace even had a garden, but it did, with a fountain. Lynn appeared with a whoosh and took a seat. She looked at the fountain as she stirred her tea.

"This brings back memories," Lynn said.

"It does?"

"I had a ton of dirty cash I had... acquired... and I needed to do something with it. With the coins at least, since they'd be hard to launder. So I just dumped them all in a fountain and made a big wish."

"Did it come true?"

"Oh, yes." Lynn grinned.

"By the way, Lynn, you must know a lot of ASL," I said. I sipped from my cup. I wasn't really a fan of caffeine, but I'd make an exception for Lynn.

"Thanks," Lynn said. "I've been studying. And I cheated a little bit: I bound a daemon to help translate."

"That's perfectly fine," I said. "As long as we can all talk."

"That's why I'm learning."

"What did you find?" I asked.

"It'd be hard to explain to a non-magister."

"Try me."

She looked around, then said "*Majikuu o kudasai*." A magic marker appeared in her hand. Invisible hands moved the tea out of the way as she drew an inscription on the table. The air outside suddenly stilled. The noise of the Palace became muted.

"Pretty cool," I said.

"It's pretty useful," she said. "Now, it's not hard to bind daemons. It's hard to bind daemons *safely*. We call it the Pyramid of Power. You need a bunch of lower-rank daemons to support the price of your high-rank contracts, and you need more even lower-rank daemons for that."

"So high-ranking daemons aren't self-sufficient?"

"We call it a closed cycle: they don't just exist. You can't bind a daemon that will support itself, or it will have no reason to let itself be bound by you. It always wants something from you. Anything." Lynn said the last word with ever so slight stiffness.

We sat in silence for a fraction of a second. "So what did you find?" I asked, to break it.

"We found evidence that something is draining the blood of those who drink the tainted water. But it's impossible that that is what the mother daemon wants, because a closed cycle is impossible."

"Wait, I thought it had disappeared?"

"It did. But a local game warden found corpses of deer and small animals drained of their blood. We did some tests and found they had the explosive protein in them." Lynn shook her head. "This is a bad sign, since it may mean something even bigger is going on. Perhaps even higher-rank daemonology."

"Oh. But I'm not sure if I understand. Why can't it feed itself with the blood? That's not a closed cycle, right? Because it has to expend effort to hunt down the animals."

"I told you it'd be hard to explain to a mundane," Lynn sighed. "It's like a perpetual motion machine. There is always something the magister provides."

"But couldn't you make a cycle of daemons that supported each other?"

"Mike, I can't explain the entire field of daemonology to you in one conversation. The short answer is no. The longer answer is that everyone who tries regrets it, dies, or regrets it shortly before their death."

"OK," I said. "Sorry."

She waved it away. "Anyway, I had to leave right away because of—well, it's a long story. Let's just say they needed a specific one of my daemons. But this does give us one clue. For whatever reason the terrorist needs to drain the blood, either because he wants to accumulate it or he does somehow need it to please the mother daemon. It's more likely than not he's really just trying to get as much of it as possible to use in a future terrorist attack. But come on, Mike, I want to spend this time with you." She snapped her fingers and the marker faded. The noise around us came back.

"So you play video games?" I changed the subject.

"Some. I barely have time for the more grindy ones anymore. But I'll play just about anything. You ever tried daemon VR?"

"Uh, no?" I asked. "I was poor."

"Come on, it's great! I'll have to show you some time."

"Great," I said.

She squeezed my hand. How wonderful it was to touch another human being. She took a deep breath. "So... we're serious, right? Seriously together?"

"Yes," I said. "Why?"

"I'm just wondering... like... where you see us in the future."

"Since the moment we became a couple, I've always been pursuing you with the intent to..." Oh my gosh did I dare say it? "Well, looking for a future marriage," I managed.

Lynn grinned ear-to-ear. "Yeah. Me, too."

I stroked her hair, touching the Imperial Diadem by accident. "When you accused Frederik about seeing you, er—"

"As being a political ally with a bonus uterus?"

"Yeah. Were you worried that I would see you that way?"

Lynn was silent for a moment. "There's... there's things you should know if we get farther than this. But this isn't the place to talk about it."

I kissed her on the cheek. "Don't worry about it. We'll take it slow. Besides, I don't care about power. I'm just some peasant who wants to see you smile."

"Aw," she said, and smiled. It seemed the world outside faded away when she looked like that. "Did anyone ever tell you you have a beautiful smile, too?"

"Aw, shucks."

"And you're so cute when you're embarrassed."

"Hey!"

She giggled and squeezed my hand. "I have a half hour left to do fun stuff. We can watch an anime, or just talk. Or maybe take a walk around the Palace?"

"That sounds fun," I said. "I don't think I've seen all of it."

"I've lived here for almost five years, and *I* don't think I've seen all of it. I keep finding new rooms. And one time I found an actual secret passage."

"You're kidding me!"

"Nope. Here, let me show it to you…"

The Judgment Games were always held in the subdominion of the punished noble. As we arrived in what was once Denmark, I saw the size of the stadium. "We had to move it," Lynn told me. "They were scalping tickets, and this was the biggest one we could find. Turns out he had a lot of enemies."

"No kidding," I said. We got out of the limo. There was something in Lynn's smug smile that chilled me more than the brisk air.

What was I worried about? I wondered as the guards passed us through before we could wave our tickets. Frederik had willingly signed up for whatever this would be, and no matter how ridiculous or humiliating, he truly deserved this. After all, it could only be a fraction of what he had done to Mom.

We climbed up stair after stair. I noticed Lynn was just hovering over the steps. "Levitation is *so* useful. By the way, did you know we're actually *in* a vomitorium right now? That's what these entrance things are called—"

"Lynn, are you taking this seriously?"

"Seriously?" Lynn asked. "What do you think these things are for?"

Before I could think of an answer, Lynn's friends waved us over to their special box. "Your Imperial Majesty!" Rafael said, waving a wineglass. "And Mike! Shame to hear about your village."

"If you want to bring them back, I have plenty of room in my dominion," Albert said.

I was disoriented for a bit. "That—that will be all right."

"I never really liked the guy," Chen told us. "All looks and no brains."

Sure, and if any of you got kicked down to commoner, the rest of you would immediately turn on him, I almost said. But I just took my seat next to Lynn.

"Something to drink?" Lynn asked me.

"I'll be fine."

"Sure? This could take a while."

"Will it?" I asked.

"Just look!"

Magisters waved their hands and chanted, and an enormous stage assembled itself on the football field. Or what I would have called a soccer field, prior to the Empire enforcing the Imperatrix's English on everyone. It was much smaller than an American football field, but the stage was still hard to see.

"Here," Lynn said. "Let's have some daemonic optics to help." She snapped her fingers. The air in front of us shimmered and suddenly I could see everything on the stage crystal clear, down to the blond beards of the magisters.

"The daemons will follow your eyes," Albert told me. "If you look at something closely, the optics will adjust."

"Hell, just use pinch zoom." Rafael said. He demonstrated with his hands in the air.

I tried it. The magisters had assembled an enormous roulette wheel and piled giant chips on the felt board next to it. One gave the wheel a practice spin, the apparently football-sized ball bouncing around inside.

All around, the vomitoria vomited crowd after crowd into the seats. Cameramen set up their cameras and magisters consulted each other.

"Ever played roulette?" Rafael asked.

"Not really," I admitted.

"You put your chips on the felt to bet, and if the ball lands on the right thing, you double your money! Or more, even!"

"Because all of the bets have less than 100% expected value, the house has an edge," Albert said.

"Yeah, and I bet you put in a twist, Lynn," Chen said.

"Of course I did," Lynn said with a sly smile. "Just wait and see."

We didn't have to wait long. Someone in a suit came on the stage. "How's it all going, everyone?" his voice boomed from the loudspeakers. "I see we got a great crowd here tonight, coming all over the world! All you highnesses and lownesses, coming to see his *former* highness's lowness—"

"He's just here to warm us up," Lynn said.

"Yeah, they should have hired a better comedian," Rafael said. He sipped, and as I looked my eyes adjusted until I could even see the bubbles in his wine. I glanced away.

In a corner, I saw two people talk with a magister. One shook his head, while another checked... a first aid kit?

People did occasionally get injured, I told myself. But I felt uncomfortable.

He left and the actual MC got on the stage. I recognized him from TV: Mark Hinerman, the host of the Judgment Games. "Welcome, everyone, to this month's Judgment Game: Electroulette! We have a very special contestant, Frederik Thorhilder, formerly crown prince of the Scandinavian Dominion!"

Frederik marched up to the stage in nothing but a thong. He strutted confidently, but I could see him slightly shiver in the cold air. The people booed. Frederik looked around with caution.

"Frederik is accused of corruption, associating with illegal organizations, interfering with the government, and oppression of the people. What do you have to say?" Mark gave him the mic.

"All lies," Frederik said. "All of them."

"Well, that's what they all say! But Her Imperial Majesty has decided to give you a second chance, if you just win 500,000 IM of chips. Ah, but you don't have any to start with."

Frederik raised an eyebrow.

"I totally thought you were going to do strip roulette here," Rafael said.

"Considering his looks, I think that would backfire," Lynn said. We all laughed.

"This game of roulette is special: you get free chips! You get to gamble 5,000 IM free for each spin," Five white chips flew over and landed on Frederik's side. "Of course, you'll have to bet all your chips each spin. But all you have to do is get 500,000 IM before that clock runs out! I should mention there's a special penalty for losing, but, ah, looks like the clock's already started."

The clock ticked from 30:00 to 29:59.

Frederik didn't waste any time, picking up the five white chips and easily hefting them to two spots on the felt. Then he hurried up to the arm of the roulette wheel and spun it with all his might. The arm spun around and slammed him back, sending him toppling.

The stadium roared with laughter. I found myself laughing, too.

"I'm curious what the twist is," Albert said. "If he bets on both red and black, the only way he can lose is if it lands on 0 or 00."

"Is there enough time? That's going to be slow," Rafael said.

Frederik got back to his feet just as the ball stopped.

"You'll see," Lynn said.

"That's a 25! You win and lose!" Mark announced.

Invisible hands moved three chips to Frederik's side and three more flew overhead and landed next to him. The other two flew away.

Then a wand flew down and struck him in the side. He screamed in pain.

"Yes, that's right! If you lose your bet, you get shocked. What a shocking twist!"

Lynn's friends cheered, and Lynn looked unbelievably smug. "See? I'm curious what he'll try now. If he hedges his bets, he'll always get zapped."

Frederik got back up, then moved his chips into place, plus five more. Five on red and six on black, I now recognized. He hurried to the wheel and spun it again.

"Because of the five free chips, he can eventually get enough if he keeps doing this," Albert mused. "But he'll only average a gain of less than 2,500 IM a spin."

I looked at the clock and the total beside it. There was no way.

The chips flew, one almost clocking him. So did the wand, prodding him in the arm. He screamed.

"This is cruel," I said.

"I know, right?" Chen said. "After what he did to you and your family…"

My stomach turned, making me glad I hadn't had anything to eat or drink.

Sure, people had sometimes been seriously injured in Judgment Games. Sure, it was *Frederik*. But as much as I hated him, this wasn't funny. This was torture!

Frederik continued betting on both sides. He didn't wince in anticipation of the wand, but he screamed every time. Then he got up and moved chips again, soon panting from the exertion.

Then the ball landed. "Whoops!" Mark said. "That's on green. You lose everything!"

Frederik didn't swear, but I could see with Lynn's optics the horror on his face as all his chips were taken away. He didn't even try to dodge the wand that time.

"Bad luck," Albert said with a sigh.

"What are the chances of him making it through with this strategy?" Rafael asked.

"I doubt he'll make it. It takes too long between spins to accumulate chips and he can lose them all in an instant."

The time ticked down. Frederik continued pilling up chips, slowly, until he had a stack. "I want to combine these chips!" he shouted.

"Sure thing!" Mark said. The chips flew around and reassembled in higher colors.

Frederik shoved a colorful stack to the inside board, then two more to other numbers, then his free chips to red and black. "High risk, high reward," Rafael said. "If he can win one spin like that…"

Frederik heaved the wheel.

"Yeah, I think that's the optimal strategy," Lynn said. "Because of the time limit."

He didn't win. Most of his chips were carried off and the wand came back, striking him on the gut. He screamed and fell.

I saw with the daemonic optics that he had lost control of his bladder.

He got up, eyes full of rage, and moved chips.

"Ten minutes left!"

He hurried faster, swinging the roulette arm with all his might.

"Does he have time?" Chen asked.

"If he gets lucky, he will," Lynn said.

He moved the chips to the inner board again, and lost them all again. He screamed in pain.

"Five minutes left!"

No. This was wrong. The thrill of seeing him suffer more and more made me physically ill.

He *didn't* deserve this.

I leaned over to whisper in Lynn's ear. "Can you cheat and make him win?"

"Why would I do such a thing?" Lynn whispered back. "It would take all the fun out of it."

"But this is cruel!"

She looked into my eyes with an expression I could not name. Not indifference, but something far worse.

"Please!" I said. "End this!"

"No," Lynn said. Still that strange expression.

"He shouldn't bother with the small bets," Albert mentioned casually. "His only chance is to hit inside bets twice."

"The chance of that?" Chen asked.

"Less than one percent. Maybe—"

I didn't listen anymore. Without thinking I found myself off my chair and running, running down the aisles and then jumping over the fencing.

I reached the stage just as Frederik lost again. He screamed. Magisters tried to block my way, but I shoved them out of it and climbed the stages. Cameras followed me.

"Hey, hold on," Mark said.

"Stop the game!" I shouted. "This is cruel!"

"No!" Frederik screamed. He was covered in sweat and tiny burn marks. He looked at me with hatred. "Keep it going!"

"Then only bet on the inside board!"

Shock dawned on his face. Then he ran to his chips and moved them all to an inside bet. Then he spun the roulette wheel.

"30! That's a win!"

Frederik looked up as the chips piled up. He almost winced, but no wand.

"One minute remaining!"

He went to the wheel, but stumbled, and finally collapsed.

I rushed to him, checking his carotid. Nothing! I shoved his chest down, again and again, until the paramedics pulled me away.

I looked at the clock. There was still time! I shoved the arm with all my might.

The wheel spun, spun, and suddenly the ball was shredded by hazy swords.

I turned to look at the royals' box. Daemonic optics showed me Lynn's face in an instant. And I saw, hiding behind the amused expression, no emotion at all.

14

Empire

They took away Frederik in a stretcher, though he was completely motion-less. "Told you electric shocks were too dangerous," a magister muttered to Mark Hinerman.

"She wanted something more extreme than usual," Mark pleaded.

The magister spotted me looking at them. He marched over. "You idiot! My daemon would have targeted you if your spin hadn't worked. And if it wasn't you, he would have shocked the contestant again."

"So you stopped it?" I asked.

He shook his head. "There's only one woman in the Empire who has Rank IIIs that look like swords."

I looked up, but the daemonic optics had stopped. I could only barely see the VVIP section.

By the time I made it back to the box, Lynn was already gone. The comedian tried to cheer us up with tasteless jokes in the background, but I wasn't listening. "Where did she go?" I asked them.

"Hell if I know," Rafael said.

"I'd text her," Albert suggested.

I got out my phone to see she had already texted me.

Head home.

I thought about it. There was no point confronting her right now, if I could even find her.

But what was that look on her face? Not even pleasure?

"Need a ride home?" Rafael offered. "Save you an Omnitaxi."

"Sure."

Bottles of alcohol lined his limo. "Want some?" he asked as we took off.

"I'm good," I said. Then couldn't I bear it anymore. "How can you just..."

"Care nothing about a former friend?" Rafael asked.

"Yes!" I snapped.

"My father was a union leader without a union. The Old Magisterium had pressured the last coal plant in the United States to close, to be replaced by a daemon-power plant they owned. No more coal power, no more power plant workers. We had nothing.

"Then the Witch-Queen came. As the nation fell into chaos, Dad found his old contacts, got together, and we took control of a city all by ourselves. Problem was, we weren't the only ones in Washington. We were one of five different revolutionary movements, two of which had magisters. We were just a large group of angry blue-collar workers.

"Her Imperial Majesty was pleased to grant us all noble titles, but only one of us could be the King of NANCD. So she ran a sumo tournament."

"A what?"

"We used inflatable sumo suits. I'm sure you've heard of them. But she was dead serious. She even had the same brackets as a real *honbasho*. My father's six-foot-five and muscular, so he won." Rafael sipped. "And so we became the royal family of the North American Northwest Coast Dominion."

"Is this about how Frederik was royal before?"

"Frankly, Her Imperial Majesty is so erratic I wouldn't be surprised if she had him go through a sumo tournament, too. But my point is that she *is* erratic. All of us are one small misstep from having our lives destroyed in an instant. Frederik was simply the latest casualty."

"I see. You realize he may be dead now?"

"He was as good as dead, anyway." Rafael said. "A royal all his life, then with actual power, then down to nothing? A goner."

I sighed.

"Yes, Mike, I didn't want to see him die. But if Lynn decided to kill him, I'm not going to argue."

I closed my mouth.

"You see, unlike the rest, you're the only person she ever gave a second chance," Rafael confided. "I thought you were doomed when you kissed her. Instead, she's still attached to you. I can't say why. But I will tell you what she wants."

"What?" I asked.

"She wants to see the people she hates suffer. Everything is a means to that end. So as long as you stay out of her way, as long as you help... then you'll have everything you want. In your case, *everything.*"

Yet—yet that was nothing like the Lynn I knew. Or had seen, behind the mask. "Everything," I repeated.

"Come on, you still haven't gone more than kisses?"

"Uh..."

"Go with the flow, man. She's obsessed with you."

"She's more than just a sex object!"

"Yes. She's also the Imperatrix Mundi and someone who will do anything for someone she loves. Enjoy it. Have fun. She could destroy you and everyone you love the moment she gets bored of you."

"Uh..."

He nudged me. "Don't tell me you haven't thought about it."

I *had*, though I wasn't going to admit it to him of all people.

"Second thoughts?" he asked.

I hesitated.

"Ah. Well, I wouldn't tell her you have cold feet. Not if you want to live. Or people in general. Breaking her heart would be bad for *all* of us. So keep her happy."

"Just stop talking."

"Sure thing, man."

I immediately went to Mom when we got back to the Capital.

The TV was on silent, but I saw the closed captioning: *...former prince was declared dead on arrival. Neither Her Imperial Majesty nor Mr. Mason could be reached for comment...* The scene replayed, a miniature me spinning the wheel, and then—I turned it off.

I was there, I signed to Mom.

I saw, she signed back. *I'm worried for you, Mike.*

She hasn't hurt me.

Mike, how much do you even know her? You've been together for three months, and you've been constantly bouncing around her life like a gumball in a gumball machine.

I don't want to break up with her! I signed angrily.

I know that. But you should really think about it. Slow down if you have to. I don't want to see you hurt or heartbroken because she turned out to be a different person than you imagined.

I shook my head. *Who is she, really?*

Why don't you ask her?

I guess I'll have to.

And pray, Mike. Pray for her every day.

I already am.

Good. Just don't assume you know what God wants out of this. If you're having second thoughts, it's time to pray about that, too.

I'm not sure what I think, anymore.

Mom hugged me, her arms barely fitting around me. *I know what it's like, Mike. I know what it's like.*

I squeezed her back. *I'll be careful. Promise.*

Lynn didn't text me again that day, nor the next, and she didn't reply to any of the texts I sent.

I called Alice. "Can we talk?"

"I was about to call you. Where are you?"

"In my apartment."

Alice appeared in a whoosh.

"Can't you use the door?" I asked.

"Do you want people to know we meet?"

"I suppose not," I said. "Is Lynn all right?"

"No," Alice said. "She won't even talk to me. I take it you haven't heard from her, either?"

I shook my head.

"I'm surprised you're even alive, to be honest."

"*What*?"

"You interfered with something Lynn set up," Alice said, still dead serious. "She was venting her anger. She'll do anything when angry. Anything. Whatever it takes to make her feel better."

But that wasn't what I saw! I almost said. She almost seemed... bored.

As if she was simply fulfilling a duty that had long since stopped being enjoyable.

But something deep within me told me not to mention that.

Alice took my silence for agreement. "I'd say she's gotten better over the years, but really she's just gotten subtler. I honestly don't think there's anything she couldn't or wouldn't do if she was just angry enough. And there's nothing to stop her. Except, now, you."

"Me?" I asked.

"Mr. Mason, the only reason Lynn is not going about business as usual is that you were involved. I don't know if she's ashamed or even more angry. Did you say anything to her?"

"I told her to stop it."

"And what did she say?"

"No."

"That's it?"

"I ran onto the field and tried to stop it, then I tried to help him when he collapsed, then..."

"But did she ask you to stop?" Alice asked, but shook her head. "No, if she wanted to stop you, she would have just sent her daemons."

"Why *does* Lynn run these games?" I asked.

"I don't know. She's never told me. And this isn't the first time someone's been seriously injured by one."

"Did she intend to kill him?" I asked.

"How am I supposed to know? She sometimes doesn't even give me her schedule." Alice set a hand on my shoulder. "But what I do know is this: there is one thing you, and only you, can do that will save the world."

"What?" I asked.

"Marry her."

"Hey, listen—"

"She wants it. I'm sure you want it. If you can stop just one of her rages..." Alice grabbed me. "We are talking about a woman who will *level cities*. How can you just sit there and do nothing? You are a *guy* for God's sake!"

"Yes, and for God's sake—"

"For God's sake, what? Why wait?" She let go. "Great. You have cold feet, don't you?"

"I didn't know Lynn was this person," I said.

"Really? You've been an Imperial Citizen for seven years and you don't know what she's like?"

I held my tongue.

"Mike, I don't care what you feel. Maybe you have cold feet. Maybe you adore her. But if you let her rampage because she didn't get to snuggle, that's on you. Do what it takes."

"Give... give me some time to think," I said.

"Think fast, then," She muttered in Latin and disappeared.

I thought about it. Time to tell someone the whole truth.

Fr. Xavier listened to my whole story without comment. "I can understand why you're so torn up," he said at last.

"I just don't know."

"Let me ask you a question," he said. "And feel free to think about it, or not to answer. But this is my question: do you love her?"

I thought about it. "I don't know. I... I want to."

"Love is willing the good of the other."

"I definitely want to see Lynn happy."

"Then you do will her good. To be frank, I've never been a fan of our current ruler, but that doesn't mean she isn't a human, deserving love and charity."

"She does," I said. "It's just that I've seen both sides of her."

"Is she a 2D object?"

"Excuse me?"

"Only perfectly flat objects have just two sides."

"I don't really know her," I said. "I thought I did, but now..."

"Then, young man, I would talk to her. Tell her how you feel. Ask her how she feels towards you. If she lies to you, then you know she's a bad match. If she tells you the truth, then you'll have to decide."

"I just want to *know* her," I said.

"We rational creatures have the utmost desire to know. What does this flower look like, what does this cookie taste like, how will the book end? Even porn is based on the desire to know. God alone can satisfy us, as the cause and end of all things. But on Earth, we must pursue the mysteries we have access to."

"I'm not sure what you mean," I said.

"You said something profound. Mysteries can be both good and bad. You want to know her? To learn her secrets? To know her as Adam knew Eve?"

"Uh..."

"It's not up to me whether any of that happens. That's between you two, and God. But the worst thing you could possibly do is to try to avoid the truth. Maybe she's meant for you and you're meant for her. I've heard stranger love stories. Or maybe, as painful as it will be, you're not meant for each other. But as long as you leave it up in the air..."

"I'll suffer," I said.

"And so will she."

I closed my eyes, took a deep breath as Lynn had showed me, and opened them. "Pray for me. I'll ask."

"You will very much be in my prayers."

I rehearsed my words as I rode up the elevator to the top of the Palace's base. I came to the security checkpoint.

"Excuse me, sir," the magister said. "Her Imperial Majesty is not currently seeing visitors."

"Tell her I'm here."

"One moment, sir," the magister said, and picked up a phone. He talked for a bit. "Yes. Yes, ma'am." He turned to me. "You may go."

I walked up the bridge, my innermost being shaking. But I was not afraid, not of the weird gravity or of what I would see at the end. I had to know. I had to learn the truth.

Or I, too, would be part of the lie.

I knocked on the door.

Lynn opened the door. Sleepless eyes regarded me for a moment. "In case you're wondering, I didn't intend to kill him. I destroyed the ball so you wouldn't be hurt. I would have let him try if he spun it. But it was just as well in the end that he died."

"What the hell, Lynn? He was your friend just a week ago!"

"He was. Maybe in another life I would have dated him. But there is one thing he is not worth, and that is the Empire."

"The Empire?"

"Follow me."

I entered after her and followed her through her apartment. We climbed up the diamond stairs.

"The Empire is always just a few days away from total anarchy," Lynn said. "Passions run high, the people demand blood: of the nobles, of me, of anyone. By giving them a scapegoat to vent their frustrations on, the Empire survives."

"Lynn, he was one of your friends."

"Was. He wasn't, after what he did to you and your village. But there's something more important than friendship. Than everything else."

We arrived at the top deck. The view was as stunning as before, but somehow all of it seemed different. Now that I knew a little of the truth, I wondered what Lynn really thought as she walked up to the railing.

"They told me I was mad," she said softly. "Why build a mobile artificial city over the ocean, when I could build a stationary one anywhere I pleased? Why not rule from historic Italian palaces—as I did, at the beginning. Why didn't I listen? Hubris? One of my more erratic moods? A childish whim? I don't know what they wondered. They never dared tell me what they really thought, other than that I shouldn't do this."

"Why did you do this?" I asked.

"Because if I had set up the seat of the Imperial Government in any one dominion, then that one would gain power over the others. It wouldn't even be intentional, most of the time. But slowly, the corruption I ripped out of the world would come creeping back in."

I thought about my words for a moment. She seemed strangely vulnerable. "I don't think you actually succeeded in ripping it out," I told her.

"You close the windows of a leaky house in the storm. My point stands."

We stood there in a silent moment. "Why?" I asked. "What does the Capital and corruption have to do with…"

"Nothing, *nothing* is more important than the Empire. I have given my entire existence to keeping it going. I am the sole woman responsible for its creation. And I am the sole woman who can stop its destruction." She looked up into the evening sky. "Do you know why I made the Empire?"

"World peace? To make the world a better place? To keep the Old Magisterium down?"

"All true enough. But do you know why of all the possible world governments, I chose an absolute dictatorship?"

"No," I admitted.

"Montesquieu laid it all out. The republic is suited for smaller nations, or leagues of smaller republics. It does not scale. The only true possibility for one universal government is an absolute despotism."

"Which you happen to be on top of," I challenged.

"No one else would do," Lynn said, unconcerned. "I, after all, fulfill the more important criteria for empress. Do you know, Michael Mason, what propels a despotism? What keeps the people, the military, the government, and the emperor all united as one?"

Michael Mason? "I don't know," I said.

She turned to me and looked fully in my eyes. "Fear," she said. "Fear is what keeps a despotism going. The people fear the military, the military fears the government, the government fears the emperor, and the emperor fears the people. Only with this cycle of fear can the world truly be at peace."

I looked back into her eyes, but could only see the Witch-Queen. "You… you aren't afraid of the people, though."

"Aren't I? Why do I have food tasters? Why do I maintain the images and actions of a tyrant? Why don't I spent all my time watching anime or playing games?" She held her hands up. "Every year or so some legal scholars take their lives in their hands and approach me with a complete model law for the Empire. Some of them were so sophisticated and ingenious that a democracy would be blessed to have them implemented. But they do not understand the most critical element of all: fear. For as long as the populace fears endlessly following afoul of one contradictory edict or another, they will remain afraid."

"You *deliberately* made the law that way?!" I demanded.

"I didn't even need to try. It's so hard to keep the Imperial Edicts straight after a while. And the nobles simply make it more complicated." She watched me with those emerald eyes, as intense as ever. "Are you afraid of me, Michael Mason?"

How could I answer? "No," I said at last.

She raised an eyebrow.

"Maybe you terrorize the world and maybe you do that deliberately, but that's not who you are. You like anime and food and, hell, even card counting."

"Tyrants can have hobbies."

"Tyrants don't cry at the ending of *Death Note*."

She turned away.

I walked up beside her. In the distance, the sun was starting to set.

"Do you want me, Mike?" Lynn asked, watching the sunset with me. "Do you want me, knowing who I really am? Not a tyrant out of necessity, but a tyrant by choice?"

"All this time you've talked about how you have no choice—"

"It is very much my choice!" Lynn snapped. "I could have exterminated the Old Magisterium and left the world to heal in peace. I could have disappeared after London fell. Some people even suggested that to me: why not simply have fun and play video games and let the world sort itself? But—" She cut herself off.

"But?"

"But this was the only option for peace." She closed her eyes.

I could tell by her slightest pause this wasn't the truth. Time to rip off the band-aid. "What's the truth, Lynn?"

She was silent.

"What's the truth?"

"Revenge," she whispered.

"Revenge?"

"On all the people that hurt me. On all the people who cruelly mistreated me. On a world that didn't give a shit about me. I took the power I needed, and made sure I was on top of the totem pole for good." Lynn sighed. "But I knew, even then, that the totem pole is a lot shakier than it looks."

"I'm sorry."

She turned to me. "Sorry? I've already told you my motives are evil. And now there's no way out. I made the Empire too useful, and deliberately destroyed the infrastructure that could be used to make the old nations return. If I let go, even for a moment, the world will fall into a civil war so bloody as to make all previous world wars seem peaceful."

"Lynn—"

"I don't have a goddamn *choice,* Mike!" Lynn shouted. "Yes, I could have made a different world. Yes, I could have brought about a happier, more peaceful world if I hadn't wanted revenge. But it's *too late.* I can't turn back history. I can't bring back the dead. The only option to keep the world from becoming hell on Earth is by keeping the existing hell on Earth going. Even if—" She stopped and looked away.

"'Even if?'"

"I'm done, Mike. If you want to go home, I'll try to get your village's situation sorted."

I took her hand. She pulled away, but turned at last. I met her grieving eyes. "I want to be with you," I said.

"Why?"

"Because no matter what you've done, no matter who you are, I love you."

Her eyes widened.

"I'm serious," I said.

"You can't be!"

"Lynn, I—"

"*EVERYONE LIES TO ME*!" she screamed. "No one tells me the truth. No one tells me how he really feels. No one!"

"Then what about this?" I asked, dropping to one knee.

She stopped, looking with even wider eyes.

"Lynn, will you marry me?"

15

The Answer

Lynn shuddered, knelt, and started crying. "You... you can't," Lynn said. "Not knowing who I am."

"Lynn," I said. "You just told me who you were. I don't care. The whole Empire can go screw itself if it has to, but I want *you.*"

"You... you want me," Lynn repeated. "You want me."

"I want you," I said.

She curled up into a ball and cried louder.

I remained kneeling.

"Everyone lies to me," she said. "Every last person. Everyone is too afraid to tell me the truth, knowing who I am."

"I've never lied to you," I promised her. "Never. And I want you."

"No one ever wanted me before, not even Sean. Not as I wanted him." She looked at me, scared. I saw in her the wounds too deep to be reached into, the child who had never been allowed to grow up. I saw, at last, who Lynn was when she wasn't the Witch-Queen.

"I want you," I said. "That's God's honest truth."

"You want me." Lynn covered her face. "You want me. You want me."

I reached out and gently stroked her hair. If only I could pull that diadem off and make her happy, I thought for an instant.

"Mike," she whispered. "There's things I need to tell you. I can't have..." She stopped. "I can't have children. It'll just be me."

Her words stabbed through me. I hadn't wanted children until I learned I couldn't have them.

But Lynn was more important.

"We can adopt," I said. "You can work out the paperwork."

"Yeah. Yeah, I can." For the first time she met my eyes. "How do I know? How can I trust you? How do I know you really want me? The real me?"

I thought about it. "Because you've shown me everything you are, and—"

"Not everything," she said. "Not everything."

"Sure, you haven't told me your secrets. But I don't care. You're not your public persona, and I think, deep down, you don't want to be."

She shook her head. "I'm trapped."

"I don't know about government and I've never read Montesquieu, but there has to be another way. There has to be some way we can keep the world running without fear. We'll find it, no matter what. Together."

"Together," she said. Then took my hand and squeezed it. "Yes, Michael Mason, I'll marry you."

My heart leapt in my throat, out of so much joy my ribcage could not contain it. I reached out and kissed her. She melted into my arms, relaxing fully as I held her.

She pushed back. "We can only do five seconds at a time," she said. "But the first thing I'm going to do is find a way we can make out all day. And more than that once we're married." She winked. "You deserve all of me."

"The first thing I want to do is get a ring on your finger."

"Of course," Lynn said, smiling. "We'll have to stop by a jeweler. But first... first, let's celebrate."

The sun finally set. We got up together and walked down to her penthouse, our hands touching as much as her daemons would allow.

Inside her apartment, as darkness fell, the diamonds began glowing.

"Did you know that artifical diamonds glow in the dark?" Lynn said. "I don't mind."

"I don't mind either," I said. I looked around, and realized that not too long from now, I would live here.

"Let's get a bit of light, though." Lynn snapped her fingers, and candles appeared and lit themselves.

We took seats across from each other at a table. "Let's celebrate." She snapped her fingers again and a bottle of champagne was carried by invisible hands to us. "France's finest." As Lynn poured some, I wondered how I would tell Mom. Or Fr. Xavier. Or Kyle. Or anyone. The whole world would want to know. "Here you go."

We clinked glasses. I felt uncomfortable, but hey, one glass on the most special day wasn't wrong. Was it?

"How long—oh my gosh, we're going to have a wedding, won't we? The biggest one in the whole world."

"All I need is you, honey."

"Yes, but we need to make it official," Lynn said. "It'll take some time to prepare—the security alone—"

"We can have it at the Basilica." I still hadn't been inside, but I had seen pictures of the massive statued interior. "We'll have guests."

"Of course. We can get your village back together for a day." She frowned. "But I want to be married soon."

"We have to go through pre-marriage counseling," I said. "It's called pre-Cana, and it's about six months."

"Oh," she said. "It's going to be the hardest six-month wait in my life."

"Me, too."

Lynn suddenly 'picked up the phone.' "I'm very busy." She scowled. "OK. I'll be there in a bit." She 'hung up.' "More terrorist activity—on the best day of my life." She started crying again.

"Lynn," I said. "This is just the best day of your life so far. We have many more best days ahead of us."

"We do." She wiped her eyes.

"The day of our wedding, our honeymoon." My mind relaxed. Alice would be delighted I would finally share a bed with Lynn, but nowhere near as delighted as I would be.

"I know just where to go for our honeymoon." Lynn winked.

"Where?" I asked.

"That's a secret." She grinned. "It's a very special place."

"All right," I said. "Then our first anniversary, and the one after that, and the one after that." What would we think, a year from now? "The day we adopt a child." What would he be like, or she? To raise a child would be an adventure all of its own.

"Sheesh, Mike, we aren't even married yet."

"There'll be one very special day, though," I said.

"What?"

"The day we figure out how to both keep the Empire together and rule the world without fear. We'll figure it out together, I'm sure of it."

"Together," Lynn agreed. She leaned in.

I leaned in, too.

We kissed.

To be continued

Acknowledgments

A book has unfortunately only one name on the cover, when so many people help with it. This has been the most collaborative book in my career.

I'd like to thank Karina Fabian, for tearing apart my book with love. Ann Lewis, whose threats of ice cream kept me going. Rena Shannon, for her enthusiasm. S. R. Crickard and Katelin Cummins, for sharing their feminine perspectives with this guy. Cesar Chacón, for sharing a guy's perspective with this guy. Rebecca W. Martin, for editing my book despite the legions of dialogue tags and the guy whose last name I never consistently spelled the same. Lisa Harmon, for her enthusiasm across genres. Brent Donoho, Zephyr Thomas, Benjamin Cheah, and Thomas Bridgeland for their insightful comments. R. M. Rose and Barbara Graver, for whom I cannot think of a witty thanking, but their encouragement and insight were invaluable. Mary Jessica Woods, Ann Moser, Patrick W. McCarthy, and Colleen Drippé, for their long-suffering patience in the doomed first draft as I figured how to write a romance novel. And the Holy Trinity, Love Itself, who opened the way to all of this.

WANT MORE WITCH-QUEEN?

You can get the latest updates by signing up to my mailing list. You'll also get the prologue to the whole series, free!

Just head over to https://bit.ly/3oMfWv1

ΔBOUT THE ΔUTHOR

M. P. Smythe has never tried to conquer the world with powerful entities beyond our four-dimensional spacetime, but he hears it has its perks. He writes adult and young adult science fiction and fantasy as Matthew P. Schmidt. When alone, he can be heard singing strange songs and contemplating fictional worlds. He lives in Martins Ferry, Ohio, with several million tiny arthropods, to many of which he is allergic.